Obedience

Volume Two

Lizzie B Brown

Contents

Message to Readers

This story was originally published to Kindle Vella and Patreon.co m/lizziebbrown. While Amazon has discontinued the Kindle Vella program, Obedience is still an ongoing story with new episodes releasing to my Patreon.

This story is not a handbook for proper BDSM. The two main characters, Joshua and Cassie, are both inexperienced. Their inexperience and how they navigate relationship dynamics they don't fully understand is the heart of the story.

This story contains: age gap (19 Years), forbidden relationships (Professor & student), light Domme/sub Themes, dubious consent, discussions of punishment, and toxic family.

This book is for all my naughty little smuts. I see you, and I thank you.

Episode 25
The Invitation

Joshua

"Maggie." I greeted her with a tight smile, hoping to hide the disgust I felt from her presence.

Maggie Ainsworth, the younger Ainsworth daughter. My chest tightened as she stood in my doorway, all smiles.

Her mother, Agnes, had a lot of influence at Pine Grove University because of her very deep pockets. The administration had no problem bending to the old bat's every whim in exchange for whatever scraps she would throw their way. Granted, they were sizable scraps but not worth some of the strings attached, in my opinion.

While not as demanding as her mother, Maggie had the same problem with the word no. Back when I first started, I made the mistake of attending one of the fundraising events they hosted for the university. Maggie took one look at me and decided I was the one, and I've been dodging her ever since.

"Aren't you going to invite me in?" she asked playfully.

"Like Margaret Ainsworth needs an invitation." The flattery felt like acid on my tongue, but I had to feign politeness.

She fluttered into my office, unaware of what had transpired minutes before. I motioned to the empty chair, offering her a seat out of obligation. If it was my choice, she would be banned from campus.

"You haven't RSVP'd for the Ainsworth Autumn Gala, Joshua." The way she stuck out her lip to pout like a child was maddening. *You're in your late thirties, dammit, act like it.*

Instead of ranting my thoughts out loud, I forced a smile.

"I never attend, Maggie. You know that. I honestly don't know why I even get an invitation each year. Your mother has no interest in my department," I said, trying to play dumb.

We both knew the reason I received an invitation to every single event put on by the Ainsworth family no matter how many times I declined. Maggie was never very good at subtlety.

"Actually, Mother has taken quite the interest recently. The most recent scholarship winner is actually an English major who transferred in."

"Really now?" I feigned interest.

"Yeah, his name is Jonathan Bailey. Bright guy."

My jaw clenched. Why did his name keep popping up? Being the Ainsworth's latest golden child meant I had to be careful dealing with him in the future. It was an open secret that their scholarship students were expected to receive preferential treatment.

"I know that name. He's in my Creative Writing class this semester," I said through clenched teeth. My cheeks burned, the muscles in my face straining to keep the faux smile in place.

Maggie leaned in, propping her elbows on the desk like she owned the place. "All the more reason you need to attend."

"Did you really come all the way here just to sway me into attending the gala, Maggie?" I asked, hoping she would finally take the hint.

"No, I'm actually on campus to pick up my niece. We have plans, but I figured I'd take care of a little business while here."

Ah, that's right. I forgot Agnes Ainsworth had a granddaughter running around campus somewhere. A few colleagues had mentioned her in passing, but I never paid attention. Agnes and Maggie were hard enough to stomach. I could only imagine what the third generation was like.

"Since you aren't going to let this go until I say yes, put me down for two," I conceded so I could be free of the conversation and her company.

"Two?" Maggie sat up, the smile dropping from her face like a dead bird mid-flight.

"Yes. Do we not get a plus-one anymore?" I asked incredulously.

While Cassie couldn't be my date, Eddie could. I needed a buffer, and he owed me after Friday night. And Saturday night. And Sunday morning, even if he *was* invited that time.

"Um, yeah. But only spouses. This is one of the more *exclusive* events," she replied sheepishly.

Dammit. Maggie was probably lying, but I knew better than to call her out on it. *Suck it up for one night, Joshua. She's not going to leave until you do.*

"Fine. I guess I'll go alone," I said begrudgingly.

"Fantastic!" Maggie leaped from her seat, clapping in excitement. "I look forward to seeing you there!"

Having accomplished her goal, Maggie said her goodbyes and vacated my office. Alone at last.

Episode 26

The Dress

Cassie

Tapping my foot, I pulled out my phone to check the time. I'd been standing next to Aunt Margaret's car for ten minutes, waiting for her to show up. To think I was worried about being the late one.

My little rendezvous with my professor left me a bit more of a mess than I anticipated. *As if any part of what happened was expecte*d. Fooling around on campus puts everything at risk, and we shouldn't have done that. But when he bolted from the classroom, I knew something was wrong and felt compelled to fix it. God knows he wouldn't have calmed himself down. *My poor professor.*

I should have stayed longer instead of making a beeline for the exit as soon as he finished. The worry ate at me even as I hastily cleaned up in the nearest bathroom. *He'll be fine.* But would he? Joshua could have easily retreated into himself once I left. My body hummed with the need to check on him.

Maybe I could rush back there real quick just to be sure. *And what will you tell Aunt Margaret?* I froze in place, unable to think up a good excuse. *Fuck!*

The last thing I needed was Aunt Margaret asking questions. Yes, she was pretty chill as far as aunts go, but I couldn't tell her about this. Even if she agreed to keep it from Grandmother, there was no way she wouldn't tell my parents. She'd personally deliver the news to them when she dragged my ass home.

I wouldn't mind the going home part, but telling my parents? I shuddered. Joshua was right around their age. I couldn't see either of them being okay with that.

Maybe a quick text—

"Sorry for making you wait," Aunt Margaret called out as she approached the car. "I thought I got here early enough to take care of business before your appointment."

Keys in hand, she clicked a button and the car unlocked.

"Business?" What business could she possibly have on campus? Grandmother was the one who liked to wield her influence and even she rarely visited the university outside of special functions.

"Following up on a few RSVPs for the gala. Speaking of, have you met Professor Porter?" She asked with a sly smile. *What is she up to?*

"Um, no?"

I kept a low profile on campus, avoiding any unnecessary inter-actions. It was easier to convince someone that I was nothing like Grandmother if they got to know me before they learned of the familial connection. If the faculty member didn't attend one of the various functions the family hosted, then they would have no idea I existed and vice versa.

"Oh, honey. We are going to have fun at the gala," Aunt Margaret gushed as she lowered into the car.

Doubtful. There was nothing fun about Grandmother parading me around like a show pony. The only saving grace was that almost no one from my major was ever in attendance. Grandmother's passions were the sciences because they bettered society. Anything art related went largely ignored.

I slumped into my seat, silently pouting as I buckled up.

"Hush with that sour look, Cassie. This year will be different." The scolding tone was in direct contradiction to the smile still curving her lips. Something was definitely up.

"How?" I asked incredulously.

"For starters, this year you can drink." She emphasized her point with a wink, drawing out a laugh from both of us as she pulled out of the parking lot.

Touché, Aunt Margaret.

—♥—

The sales lady at Champagne Blush poked and prodded me, her perfectly manicured fingers making no attempt to be gentle. I hated this place and the unwelcoming atmosphere it created, but it was Grandmother's favorite for some reason.

Because the staff is as cold as her heart. I fought back a snort, the idea tickling me with how true it was. The sales associates were all old and void of any genuine emotions. It was a wonder they stayed in business.

"This blue looks lovely on her," the woman remarked with a dead smile that didn't reach her eyes.

She knows you're an outsider. They all do. If Aunt Margaret wasn't with me, I wouldn't be allowed past the front door. Even if everything went according to my mother's plans, I would never be rich. The light at the end of this hellish tunnel was a comfortable living at best. Fine by me. Much to Grandmother's disappointment, every attempt to woo me into her life of wealth and privilege only pushed me further away.

"Yes, Mother did a great job picking this one," my aunt remarked.

Record scratch. Grandmother picked this out?!

Based on the plunging neckline and the slit all the way up my thigh, I assumed Aunt Margaret picked out the dress. It screamed sex, something the great Agnes Ainsworth never did. Something wasn't right.

I shot Aunt Margaret a look of concern in the mirror's reflection. A neutral mask fell over her features as our eyes met. Her ability to slip it on so easily was almost concerning. *Until you meet her mother.*

"Give us a moment, Odette," she said, dismissing the other woman.

"Of course, Miss Ainsworth." Odette gave a small bow before pulling back the curtain and rushing off.

I silently counted to ten, wanting to give the sales lady enough time to vacate the vicinity before losing my cool. Call me paranoid, but I didn't want my private conversations getting back to the bitch.

"What are you not telling me?" I demanded in a whispered sort of yell.

Aunt Margaret rolled her eyes as she waved her hand in the air. "Stop being dramatic. Be happy you get a dress you'll actually wear again this time."

Moments like this reminded me that despite being the exact opposite of Grandmother, my aunt still grew up in a world of privilege that was very different from my own. She probably had a closet full of dresses like this, never wearing the same one twice.

"Where would I possibly wear *this* again?" I asked, motioning to the silky blue dress I was encased in.

Was the dress beautiful? Stunningly so. But that didn't change the fact that my nights out were spent at Burger Dan's or on my couch.

"I don't know. Look, you haven't brought anyone special around and she's getting impatient. We both know you'll never bring a man within ten feet of that woman, but she doesn't. Just play along until she loses interest. Okay?" Aunt Margaret gave me an exasperated look.

Okay wasn't even close to how I felt. As if she didn't already make my college life difficult enough, Grandmother wanted to pimp me out at the gala next weekend. The place would be crawling with faculty, alumni, and scholarship students. No one would take me seriously if I showed up dressed like some rich man's sugar baby.

At least *he* wouldn't be there to watch me demean myself. That thought offered a little comfort.

Aunt Margaret stepped closer and pulled me into a hug. My shoulders sank as I leaned into her embrace.

"I know, honey, I know. Your mom and I have both been there. She eventually loses interest in meddling. I promise," she whispered into my ear.

"How did you make her stop?"

"Oh, darling. It was easy." She took a step back. "After your mom ran off, your grandmother feared I would do the same. She planned this lovely intimate dinner and invited only potential suitors of her choosing. It was mortifying how obvious she was about the whole thing. But you know what I did?"

"What?"

"I openly flirted with every single man at the table *and* the caterers," she confessed. The sparkle in her eyes was downright devious, as was the wicked grin she flashed me.

"No. You. Didn't," I said in disbelief.

Since being shipped off to Grandmother and Aunt Margaret, I had only ever seen her act the dutiful daughter around her mother. Any acts of defiance had always been behind the scenes. Her story went against everything I knew.

"I did, and it was glorious. Your grandmother was so embarrassed that she let it go for a bit. She tried again some years later, but quickly backed down when I pretended to seduce a long-time friend of the family. You have to be clever about these things, Cassie." She made it sound so simple.

"And how do I be clever about this dress?"

"The way I see it, you now have a beautiful dress to wear after graduation when you dramatically announce you are cutting her off," she answered with a shrug.

That... that wasn't a bad idea.

I squeezed her in thanks before letting go to look at my reflection again. Who knows, maybe I needed to take a page of Aunt Margaret's playbook. Not at the gala where I needed to keep my reputation at least somewhat intact, but it might prove useful in the future.

Episode 27
Taco Tuesday

Joshua

A soft knock on my office door pulled my attention from the papers I was grading. *Great, another distraction.* The plan was to spend Tuesday afternoon grading papers for Creative Writing, but the stack wasn't shrinking. Ten wasn't that many, but I couldn't focus worth a damn today. The entire office reminded me of Cassie and how it felt to bury my cock in her. Every time I looked at my desk, I imagined her bent over, ass in the air, demanding I fuck her. Maybe next time she would let me wrap her blonde hair around my fist while I made her scream. My cock stirred, begging me to go home and show it some attention.

"Professor Grant?" an unfamiliar voice called from the other side of the door. Unfamiliar and... male?

Who could that possibly be? I didn't have any appointments scheduled.

May as well entertain whoever it is. It wasn't like I was getting any work done anyway.

"Come in," I called out.

The door opened, revealing a man I had never seen before dressed in jeans, a collared shirt with the sleeves rolled up, and a sweater vest. The ensemble looked more professional than the students dressed, but he was definitely younger than me.

Relief washed over his features as he entered the office and laid eyes on me.

"Thank God you're here," he said.

We stood silently as I waited for the stranger to introduce himself and explain why he was here. He stared back at me, oblivious to the awkwardness of the quiet that surrounded us.

"Um, can I help you...?"

"Oh, yes! Sorry, we haven't been introduced yet." He took a few steps forward, extending a hand as he introduced himself. "Zack Porter, new professor in the history department."

Professor Porter? He looked so young. *So did you in the beginning.*

I stood, holding in a wince as we shook. It has to be one of the oddest handshakes I had ever experienced. His grip was firm and his palms a tad damp. I tried not to hide my unease as I pulled my hand back.

"You can call me Joshua. It's a pleasure to meet you." I offered Zack a seat, motioning to the chair on his side of the desk before taking my own.

"Great. Joshua. Thank you. I was advised you would be the best person to talk to."

Despite the bright smile on the man's face, something was off. His hands fidgeted in his lap while his right leg bounced a mile a minute.

"About? I can't imagine being useful to anyone in the history department. Not really my thing," I replied with a chuckle, hoping to ease whatever tension he was hiding.

"Actually, it's about the students. How do you make them stop? They are so brazen. It's terrifying. Yesterday, I had a random girl offer to carry my children. She's not even in any of my classes!" he explained.

I held back a wince, remembering what it was like when I first started.

"How did you respond?" I asked.

"I froze. I fucking froze! I mean, who uses *that* as their pickup line?" Zack ran a hand over his face while releasing a long sigh. "At some point, I think I muttered 'I'm child-free, sorry' and walked away."

Laughter erupted as I pictured the scene. It felt good knowing I wasn't the only one suffering. *Though no one has offered to have your kids yet.* Thank God.

Zack gave me a crooked smile, running a hand through his dark hair as his gaze fell to the ground. He was putting on a brave face, but I could see the defeat in his eyes. *Look familiar?*

I straightened in my chair, immediately regretting my reaction. He needed a friend, or at least a place to feel safe. God knows I could've used an ally when I first started.

"Sorry to laugh, man. I just haven't heard that one before."

"No, I get it. The crazy thing is, I'm used to being hit on. I just, I don't know. I never thought students would be so forward."

"Wait until they call you daddy," I replied.

"I'd rather not," he said with a grimace. "So, how did you make it stop?"

Zack leaned forward, eagerly waiting for me to divulge some great secret that didn't exist. I felt bad that I couldn't offer him what he wanted.

"I didn't," I confessed. "Hate to break it to you, but it still happens fairly regularly. But the administration is good about taking care of things if you bring it to their attention. Just document everything so you have something to reference if you need them to intervene. And try to never meet with a student alone. Have a witness, always."

His shoulders slumped as he leaned back in the chair. The despondent stare he cast towards the floor sucked any joy out of the room. It was like looking in a mirror, a very depressing mirror. There was only one thing to do in a situation like this.

"Tell me, Zack, how do you feel about Taco Tuesdays?"

My face scrunched as the sour post-shot lime did little to cover the bitterness of the tequila. While not my favorite alcohol for a plethora of reasons, most of which escaped me at the moment, you couldn't have Taco Tuesday without tequila.

"That was the last one. Five is my limit," I announced.

The shot glass made a clink as I slammed it onto the table with more force than intended. Whatever. It was fine. Everyone was too enthralled with the mariachi band at the opposite end of the restaurant to care about my folly.

Zack let out a smirk, shaking his head before grabbing a taco and taking a big bite.

"Dude, that was our seventh," he corrected me, mouth still half full of food.

Oops.

We gave each other a look before bursting into a mutual fit of laughter. Our gleeful noise caught the attention of a few nearby patrons, who glanced towards our booth. Normally, the attention would bother me, but I was riding the warm, fuzzy wave of tequila. Very little could bother me at that moment.

"Oh well, I can always get a Lyft home and grab my car later."

Zack nodded, a big smile plastered on his face. The weight of our initial conversation dissipated a few shots ago, leaving us to enjoy the hearty plate of tacos on the table.

I grabbed myself some of the crunchy goodness and took a bite, moaning a little as the seasoned beef filled my mouth. Drunk taco time was the best. Freshman year of college, Eddie and I spent almost every Tuesday doing shots, eating tacos, and working our way through the waitresses. *Eddie had you beat on the waitresses.* Only because sleeping with a new girl every week has never been my style. I could have easily pulled more than him. *Fuck, I'm drunk.*

"Please don't take this the wrong way, but I've had too much tequila for you to make that sound," Zack said, interrupting my internal ramblings. His eyes were cast down at the table, a faint blush spread over his cheeks. *Weird.*

"What sound?" I asked before taking another bite.

"That. It sounds like you and the taco are getting pretty intimate. As pleasant as it is, you are a bit too old for me," he quipped.

"I wish the students felt that way about me," I started to lament before the words soaked into my tequila addled brain. " Wait, did you just say—"

"Shots please," Zack called out, cutting me off.

The server nodded as she passed.

"Um, Zack..." I trailed off, unsure what to say.

We sat in silence while I tried to process what I was feeling. Was I mad? Uncomfortable? No. Well, maybe?

"Sorry. I didn't mean to say it out loud. I'm not going to make a pass at you, if that is what you're worried about." The entire apology, he kept his eyes on his hands as he fidgeted.

Being upset seemed pointless. He was clearly embarrassed. *And buzzed*. Yes, and buzzed. We both were.

"That has to add a whole different level when they hit on you, huh?" I offered, hoping to ease some of the weird tension.

"Huh?" Zack's head shot up, a look of confusion as he digested my words. The expression slowly faded as his eyes grew wide and a smile broke free. "I like women, too. Just ones my own age. On both fronts."

On both fronts? What did that even—oh! Something clicked into place as I realized what he was saying.

"Oh... Oh!" I sputtered like an idiot.

Your new friend tells you he's bi and you start chanting "oh." Good one, Joshua. The cringe feeling burned more than the tequila or jalapeno salsa. *Fuck.*

"Yep," he said, popping the P sound at the end. The mood at our table shifted to something far different from the discomfort of our initial meeting. I couldn't tell if he was still embarrassed, or uneasy because of my lame reaction.

"I've made this weird," he followed up. "This whole transition and new job have been one clusterfuck after another."

His confession, while misplaced, tugged at my heartstrings.

"You didn't make this weird," I insisted.

"Yeah, right."

"No, I'm serious. Weird is when my friend Eddie burst in on me naked in my kitchen over the weekend. Promise not to do that, and we are fine."

Zack stared for a moment, silently grasping for words that never came.

"Okay... I think I can handle that," he finally managed.

The server stopped by at that moment with more shots and a pitcher of water. Without hesitation, I grabbed one and downed it, eager to blur the current conversation away. Zack laughed, downing his shot after.

"So, tell me more about what happened with Eddie."

The ride home went better than expected. After shot number eight, Zack and I switched to water and nachos to work through the worst of it. By the time the ride I ordered arrived, most of the fog had cleared from my mind. Yes, my head still swam a little, but I could walk in a straight line. Sort of.

I was stepping out of the elevator when my phone buzzed in my pocket. Swiping it unlocked, I was greeted with the sweetest sight, a message from my Goddess.

Cassie: Home?

I tried to tap out a reply, but my thumbs wouldn't do as they were told. Despite my eagerness to reply, I was too buzzed to text and walk. *Just have to wait until inside.* And maybe another glass of water, if I was being honest with myself.

I pulled out my keys as I turned the corner, dropping them a few feet from my door in shock.

"Cassie?"

Episode 28

Dropping By

Cassie

Standing outside Joshua's door, I tried to remember why I thought stopping by unannounced was a good idea. Five minutes had passed since I last knocked and still no answer. *Maybe he had plans...*

I whipped out my phone and shot him a quick text. Worst case, I would just catch a ride to Aunt Margaret's and crash there for the night.

Or go home.

No, home was not an option. Nicole decided last minute to host a little gathering. I was all on board until she mentioned Jonathan would be in attendance. The issue would have been resolved days ago if I took the direct approach and stated that I wasn't interested in no uncertain terms, but the coward's path was easier. Or I thought it was, but standing outside the professor's apartment I wasn't so sure.

The jingle of keys followed by a thud startled me as someone rounded the corner.

"Cassie?"

Joshua stood two arms' lengths away, staring at me like he couldn't believe I was real. Or maybe he was scared? I probably interrupted his plans, though I'm not sure what plans they would be since he was still in the same clothes as earlier.

"Hello." I greeted him with a sheepish grin and a tiny wave.

Confusion gave way to hunger as Joshua stalked closer. A few steps in, he began to sway as if he treaded on uneven terrain. *Strange.* The obstacle did little to deter him, proving to be a mild inconvenience at most.

My concerns were soon forgotten as the scent of cumin and lime danced around me. Visions of tacos and salsa made my mouth water almost as much as the sexy man who drew closer.

"Someone had Mexican," I remarked.

Joshua tugged me into his arms, wrapping me in his warm embrace. "Mm-hmm. Had dinner with a friend." He leaned in and whispered against my skin.

His hands drifted down my back to the hem of my shirt, then back up under the fabric. Goosebumps broke out over my skin as his hands roamed freely.

"Eddie?" The name came out as more of a moan than a question.

A low rumble of displeasure vibrated through Joshua's chest until a growl escaped.

"Never say his name like that. In fact, don't say his name at all. Forget he exists," Joshua warned.

"*Or?*" I challenged, pulling away from his hold.

He huffed, grumbling under his breath, as he tried to pull me back into his embrace, but I sidestepped to thwart his attempt. As hot as I found Joshua's jealousy and possessiveness, I wasn't about to let him cross the line into red flag territory. Poor behavior needed to be nipped in the bud early on.

"Or I'll have to make you forget any man's name, but mine," he said. It was a dark, delicious promise that had my pussy wet and needy.

I let out another soft moan as he dropped to his knees, slowly kissing the denim fabric covering my thighs. *Why the fuck did I wear jeans instead of a skirt?* My fingers laced through his salt and pepper hair as I guided him toward my center. I ached for the feel of his tongue as he licked until my bones were jelly and my mind fogged with contentment.

"I'm going to make you scream my name so loud there will be no question who owns your pleasure," he declared. I wanted that. God, did I want that.

Stop it, Cassie. You are the one in charge, not him. That's right. As much as I wanted what the professor was offering, it had to be on my terms.

My first attempt to stop the ravishing only caused his hands to tighten around my ass and grunt. The man was determined, but so was I. With a firm grip, I yanked him by the hair.

"Naughty, Professor. Someone might need a little *discipline*."

The threat stopped Joshua dead in his tracks. He looked up at me with the lost puppy expression I adored so much.

"I'm sorry, my Goddess. I don't understand. Why?"

His confusion caught me off guard. Something was wrong. Joshua was the cautious one. It usually took a bit of prodding to make him forget his surroundings. He shouldn't have been so eager to take me out in the open.

"I don't want to be tongue fucked in the middle of your hallway where your neighbors might see," I replied.

His face fell as he looked around us.

"I—I didn't—*Fuck!*" Joshua stumbled over his words as he tried to stand.

He wobbled the first few attempts to get to his feet, bracing himself against an unknown force. I lent a hand, helping him balance until he was steady.

"You're not acting like yourself. Is everything okay?" I asked as he wobbled again.

"Yes, I'll be fine. The floor is still rocking, though. I thought it would be done by now," he explained.

The floor is rocking? The only way the floor would be rocking was if he was—

"*Professor*, are you drunk?" I asked, unable to hide my shock. *God, I sound like my parents.*

Joshua rubbed the back of his head while flashing me a grin. "Apparently."

That explained a lot.

The grin faded as he patted his pant pockets, searching for something. "Wallet, phone, but where are my—"

Walking over to where Joshua dropped his keys, I bent down to retrieve them. He mouthed an adorable *thank you* as I walked past him and unlocked the door.

There was something comical about seeing one of my professors drunk. *But you don't bat an eye at the thought of fucking him.* This was different. I never associated sex with irresponsibility. Drinking to the point that the floor rocked beneath you was as far from responsible as you could get on a Tuesday night.

I made it two steps in the door before Joshua pinned me against the wall with his body. Warm hands slid under my top, groping my breasts through the thin lace layer of my bra.

"Fuck, how is your body so perfect?" Joshua groaned as he rolled his hips, rubbing his erection against my leg.

"Are you always this horny when drunk?" I asked, panting for breath.

My body sparked to life with every hungry touch as he explored like a clumsy teenager. While the change in confidence was amazing, his inability to focus on any one part of me for more than a few seconds was driving me insane. The need to be stripped down and fucked hard eroded my self-control.

"What makes you think it's the alcohol that has me so worked up?" Joshua whispered, nipping at my ear.

"Because," I said as I placed my hand on his chest and pushed, "it usually takes a bit more coaxing to get you to play."

Joshua took the hint, taking a few steps back. His eyes trailed down my body as he pulled his bottom lip between his teeth. The way he blatantly fucked me with his eyes was so unlike my professor.

"I think I was more than eager the last time you were here, as were you."

The smart retort I had ready to go vanished as Joshua removed his shirt. For a man with salt and pepper hair, he was still in incredible shape. The smug asshole smirked as my eyes zeroed in on his lickable abs as if he knew exactly what I was thinking. Maybe he did, and that was the point.

Oh... The professor has moves. He's been holding out on me.

As hot as it was watching Joshua display some much-needed con-fidence, it all started to feel a little too much like the cocky men of my past. If we were going to play, then it needed to be on my terms, not his.

A smile curved my lips as I stalked toward my prey. *That's right, Cassie, think sexy lioness.* His eyes darkened as arousal pooled between my thighs. *Don't worry, Professor. You'll get a taste.*

Placing a hand on his shoulder, I guided Joshua to the ground. He dropped to his knees without hesitation, almost eager to kneel before me.

"Good boy," I cooed as I ruffled his hair.

"Only for you, Goddess."

Episode 29
Control

Cassie

There is something incredibly sexy about a man kneeling before you. It is even sexier when that man is your college professor.

Despite the attempt to take charge only moments ago, Joshua held his position on the floor obediently. His heated stare followed me as I removed my shoes and walked farther into the apartment.

"Come along," I urged when he didn't immediately follow me into the living room.

Relief washed over me as I watched him slowly get to his feet instead of crawling. It might be fun to make him crawl in the future, but I wasn't ready for that.

"Your couch is so comfy," I said as I plopped down.

Joshua smiled, pleased that I made myself at home in his space so easily. That would be such a Joshua thing to think.

As soon as I settled myself, Joshua dropped back down to his knees and laid his head on my lap. I almost offered him a space on the couch but held back. This was something he needed if he resumed without prompting.

He wants comfort. I could do comfort.

I scratched Joshua's head as he wrapped his arms around my legs and nuzzled my thighs, the scruff on his cheeks scratching against the denim. A quiet peace settled between us. I'd never experienced anything like it, at least not with a guy. There was no rush to fill the silence with pointless noise. We just sat and existed in the same space, enjoying being together.

Joshua released a sigh of contentment with a dopey, drunk grin still on his face. "I'm happy you're here..."

"But?" Something about the way he said it, I knew there was a but.

Joshua's brow furrowed as he let out a little huff. "*But...* why? Is everything okay?"

Of all the things he could have said, that was last on my list. I could have told him I was avoiding Jonathan, but the little voice in my head warned me not to. *He's already aggressive towards Jonathan. If he knows you're upset, he might get involved.* That wouldn't be good, for the professor or for me.

"Everything's fine. I just missed you," I said.

His eyes narrowed, my sweet smile doing nothing to ease his suspicion.

"Liar. I won't make you talk, but I'm here if you need it."

He tightened his embrace around my legs, anchoring himself. *No, wait. This is different.* The little voice in my head was right. The professor wasn't trying to seek comfort; he was giving it. A smile crept over my lips as the realization filled me with warmth.

"I'm sorry for dropping by unannounced," I said.

"I'm not."

Of course he's not.

"Still, what if you had company?" *What if it was someone from work?* I didn't want to ruin Joshua's chill mood, but the longer I dwelled on my choice to show up unannounced, the dumber it seemed.

"You and Eddie are the only people I have over, and he is rarely the one to make the drive." He sighed, closing his eyes.

The innocuous remark made my heart break a little. Part of me knew he didn't have a large group of friends. He never talked about anyone, but I told myself he was just trying to keep me separate. The way he talked as he lay on my lap made it sound like he only had Eddie.

"Is that who you were out with? How far did you drive like this?"

"I was out with a new colleague for Taco Tuesday. Called a ride to bring me home," he explained, somewhat distracted.

"Oh..." *Colleague? Not friend?* "Did you have fun?"

Joshua shrugged. "I got hit on and rejected at the same time. That was a bit weird, but we had fun overall."

Hit on? By who? The mystery colleague? Colleague implied the same level, right? So probably not the administration staff. Were any of the professors sexy women?

No, stop it. He's with you, Cassie. Damn straight he was, and I intended to prove it.

With a firm grip, I curled my fingers in his hair. Arousal coursed through me as I watched Joshua's body relax in my hold. He gazed up at me with hungry, hooded eyes, drunk on more than booze. *The professor likes it a little rough. Interesting.*

The energy swirling between us was delicious, but it carried a weight with it I hadn't felt before. He wasn't resisting me or hesitating like he had in the past. No, he was acting on instinct. That knowledge made my pussy wet and needy. Good thing I had a way to relieve the ache growing between my thighs.

"Still hungry, *Professor*?" I asked in a husky voice.

His eyes trailed down my body to where my thighs were squeezing together. *Such a smart man.*

"Always, my Goddess," he rasped, licking his lips.

I kept my hold on him as he peeled off my jeans and tossed them aside. I needed the connection of my power over him. He let out a groan as I parted my legs, giving him a better view of my lace panties.

"Fuck, so beautiful," he whispered as he leaned in.

The adoration in his eyes left me feeling both desired and constricted. I wasn't some object to be admired from afar. Objects had no agency. No power. I was a queen on her throne to be served. No, I was a goddess to be worshiped.

My grip tightened as I kept him from leaning closer.

"No talking," I ordered. "Your only job is to lick me until I come all over your face."

Nice one, Cassie. Way to talk dirty and *take charge.*

Joshua nodded in understanding, or tried to. My hold made it difficult for him to move. *Oops.*

Releasing my hold on his hair, I stood and slowly slipped my underwear off. Joshua knelt patiently in front of me, mesmerized. *He really does find me beautiful.*

Plenty of girls on campus ogled him, a few were even bold enough to hit on him, but he had never shown interest in a single one. Nicole filled me in on everything the moment she knew I was in his class.

She even pulled up some club online full of horny students lusting after him. *And he only has eyes for me.*

Seated back on the couch, I spread my legs and pulled his face to my waiting core. I never needed a man's tongue the way I needed his. Probably because the others were never any good at it, not like Joshua.

With his hands on my thighs, Joshua ate me like a starved man who had just been offered a grand feast. I wiggled and writhed with every sweet flick of his tongue as sparks of pure pleasure exploded through me.

Eyes closed, I threw my head back and moaned out his name loud enough that his neighbors likely heard me. That sent Joshua over the edge as he doubled his efforts, adding two fingers into the mix. *Fuck, yes!*

The pressure built as his tongue circled my clit, swirling me closer and closer. My thighs squeezed his head as I gripped the back of the couch for dear life. *So fucking close.*

My body flooded with sudden warmth as my orgasm slammed into me. Joshua's fingers dug into my flesh as the hand holding me kept my hips from rising off the couch. The pain mixed with pleasure sent me flying higher than I ever had before.

Joshua waited until I stopped pulsing around his fingers to give me a reprieve. We were both panting, exhaustion taking its hold.

I stared up at the ceiling, absolutely lost in my post orgasmic high. No man would ever live up to what I just experienced. Professor Grant ruined me.

"Good...boy," I praised between heavy breaths. *Very good boy.*

Silence.

I turned my attention from the ceiling to the man that rocked my world. He stared at his lap with brows furrowed and a frown on his face. *That's not concerning at all.*

"Joshua? Is everything okay?"

Episode 30

The Morning After

Joshua

The alarm on my phone assaulted my ears with a steady beeping sound that was clearly designed to drive a man insane. Most mornings I could handle the noise, but after a night filled with tequila and tacos, I was not in the mood.

Should have turned it off before crashing last night. Should have, could have, would have would not stop the damn blaring.

Just because I wasn't dying from a major hangover didn't mean I was symptom free. I would definitely need a few aspirin and a tall glass of water when I finally rolled out of bed. And Tums. Lots of Tums.

"Fucking phone," I grumbled as I blindly smacked around the nightstand.

The screeching noise mocked me as I repeatedly grabbed at nothing. Morning class was not happening today. Maybe not the afternoon one, either.

"Your phone is the devil," Cassie said while groaning.

Cassie...

I froze as memories of the rest of the night resurfaced. Cassie waiting for me outside my door... eating her out on my couch... coming in my pants like a teenager. *Fuck.* My cheeks heated as the embarrassment came flooding back with a vengeance.

Beeeeep. Beeeeep. Beeeeep. Beeeeep. Beeeeep. Beeeeep.

The damn alarm wasn't helping my state of mind, either. With one last attempt, my hand finally grasped the little terror. I quickly powered off the phone, too unfocused to figure out the alarm. *Can't torment me without any power.*

"My hero," Cassie murmured as she wrapped her arms around me.

The feel of her flesh pressed against mine made me very aware of just how naked we were under the blanket. I could feel my cock stir as she ground her slick pussy against my side. *Someone's horny.*

"Feeling any better this morning?" she asked between soft kisses.

Despite the minor throb in my head, my body still reacted to her every touch. I doubt it was possible to be sick enough that I'd be immune to the carnal whims of my sweet Goddess.

"About last night—" I tried to explain, only to have Cassie cut me off.

"Don't worry about it, Joshua. You didn't kick me out. We all get weird when we drink."

"Why would I kick you out?" I asked. Scanning through my memories from last night, I tried to think of something, anything, that might have given her that impression.

"I don't know. One minute you are giving me an amazing orgasm, the next you are all frowny. You wouldn't talk to me even after you abruptly excused yourself to change. I would have pushed it more last night, but I wasn't sure if it was the alcohol or something else... and I didn't feel like going home."

It took a moment for her explanation to sink in. That wasn't how I remembered last night. *No more tequila, Joshua.*

"I'm so sorry," I said, pulling her into my arms. "I got a little too excited and made a bit of a mess in my, um, pants. I was embarrassed. I never meant to make you feel bad."

The room fell quiet. It was an oppressive silence that ticked by slowly as I waited for Cassie to laugh.

"Wait, was that all?" she asked, breaking the silence. Her response left me more than a bit miffed.

"What do you mean, *is that all*?"

Cassie shrugged in my embrace. "I don't know. I thought maybe I didn't react right, or you wanted me to leave after you got some and were mad I wasn't taking the hint. I thought something serious happened."

"How is me blowing my load in my pants not serious?" I demanded, more confused than angry. This entire conversation felt insane.

"You were humping your couch like a horny puppy, so it's not all that surprising. Honestly, it's kind of a compliment."

"How is it possibly a compliment?"

The normally alluring mirth of Cassie's giggling grated on my nerves as it filled the room. Being laughed at was exactly what I had hoped to avoid.

"Let me turn this around. What if I came while giving you a blow job?"

"That would be incredibly sexy." Just picturing her face twisted in ecstasy while she sucked me off was enough to have the blanket tenting.

"Exactly," she agreed, as if that made everything better.

"It's different, though," I tried to argue. Her pride isn't hurt if she orgasms too soon, but that probably wouldn't hold much water with Cassie.

"It's not, but even if it was, who cares? I don't. I hate how you get down on yourself for things that don't feel like real problems. I mean, not to belittle what you perceive to be a problem, but you know what I mean." Cassie let out a frustrated huff.

I couldn't stop myself from chuckling at her tangent. *Is that what I sound like?*

"Whatever," she said, grabbing a pillow and hitting me with it.

After a long, hot shower and some aspirin, I started to feel like myself again. I was tempted to drag Cassie in with me for some fun, but my little shower would have been far too cramped.

While Cassie was in the shower, I put in an order for breakfast to be delivered. It would be nice to take her out on a proper date, but being seen together in public was a horrible idea. If someone recognized me, it would mean a lot of trouble for the both of us.

Heaviness crept into my heart at the realization this would never be a normal relationship. It would be a few years before we could be seen in public together, assuming we lasted that long. We'd been giving this a go for only a week. It was foolish to start thinking long term.

The reality was we were on borrowed time. Soon, Cassie would meet someone who wouldn't have to hide her like a dirty secret. He would be able to take her on dates and show her off to his friends. I would be left alone, again.

You can show her off to your friends. Not out in public. *Not out in public here, but elsewhere...*

A picture of a happy couple stuck to my fridge with a magnet, George and April's wedding invitation. George was one of my dear friends from high school with whom I still kept in touch. In fact, the rental Eddie procured over the summer belonged to George.

Pulling the invitation off the fridge, I took a moment to read over the details.

April Gladstone & George Austin
request the honor of your presence
at their wedding on the 31st of December
at seven in the evening.
The Driftwood Inn
Olympus, Florida
Dinner & dancing to follow.
Attire is beach formal.

No. *Yes.* Maybe. *You could take her around town, out in the open. Make a vacation out of it.* I mulled over the idea. Bringing Cassie as my plus-one would definitely turn some heads, though not for the right reasons. *No one would know she's your student.* But they'd be able to guess. My friends knew my profession. *Your friends wouldn't report you.*

I spent what felt like forever going back and forth on the issue before tabling it. The RSVP deadline wasn't until November, so I had plenty of time to decide. With the invitation back on the fridge,

I turned my attention to more pressing matters, like spare clothes for Cassie.

Episode 31
Learning Curve

Cassie

I should have packed an overnight bag. Rummaging through the bathroom cabinets, I found all the same items as last time. Professor Grant was the typical man—basic soap, no lotion. Honestly, I was surprised he had real shampoo and conditioner and not one of those two in one combos. *Or three in one that included the body wash.* I shuddered at the thought.

The steam that still filled the bathroom clung to my skin, leaving a damp sheen despite my best efforts to dry off. I ran the towel over my body one last time before conceding it was a lost cause. Losing the battle with the moist air was almost enough to distract from the lack of toiletries in the professor's cabinets.

Hop online and order some things to be delivered. Would that be too forward? We'd barely been together for two weeks. But this was my second morning waking in his bed, and it would probably happen more often considering we couldn't go out in public. If I gave him a heads up, maybe it wouldn't seem weird.

Wrapping a towel around my hair, I walked the short distance from the bathroom to the bedroom. The cool air in the hallway was a stark contrast to the muggy bathroom. My skin pebbled as my nipples tightened from the drop in temperature.

I could have wrapped a second towel around my body, but then I wouldn't have had the pleasure of Professor Grant's overexaggerated reaction when he caught me. *Joshua*, the voice in my head reminded me, *he likes to be called Joshua*. I tried to be good about it in my head, but I preferred Professor Grant. There was something forbidden about using his title that got me all twisted up inside. In a good way, of course.

I barely made it to the door when the professor, *Joshua*, stumbled upon me. His mouth dropped open, eyes widening, as if he'd never seen me naked before. The shock only lasted a few seconds before he faked a cough, attempting to regain his composure.

"Um, did you need another towel? I have plenty," Joshua offered with a frown.

The professor's compulsion to care for me, while sweet, was not the kind of attention I sought at the moment. If he needed a little push to play, I could do that. Turning from the doorway, I positioned myself so he had an unobstructed view of my body. A smile tugged at the corners of my lips as he fought to maintain eye contact. It was a cute reminder of how reserved sober Joshua could be.

"If I want to cover my body, I can use this one," I said, reaching for the towel on my head and unraveling it.

Instead of wrapping it around my body like he expected, I reached out my arm and dropped it to the ground. Joshua relaxed, finally getting the message. No longer worried about whatever held him back, he let his eyes slowly wander over my body, licking his lips as he soaked in the view.

"You enjoy teasing me, don't you?" he said with a smirk.

"I enjoy making you *want* me, Professor," I corrected.

He looked back up at my face, his expression suddenly unreadable. "I always want you. Always. It's becoming a bit of a problem."

That wasn't the response I was expecting. *When is it ever with the professor?*

"Why is wanting me a problem?" I combed my fingers through my blonde hair, trying to distract myself from the unease his words created.

Joshua took a few steps closer, locking me in place with his intense stare. He had quite a bit of charisma and power at his command, though I wasn't sure he knew that. If he really wanted to flip things upside down, there was a chance I would submit all too willingly.

"Because you're my student and nineteen years too young and I shouldn't want you, but I do. Watching you in class and not being able to touch you is absolute torture. All I want to do is worship your body with mine. Do you not see the problem with any of that?" The words were a seductive whisper that sent a shiver of arousal through me.

He kept prowling toward me as he spoke, a dark desire painted over his features. His confession had my knees weak and my core throbbing. I tried to stand tall and pretend I wasn't affected, but it was becoming more and more difficult the closer he got.

Maybe taunting him while I was naked wasn't the smartest decision. *Or maybe it was...*

"No, I don't," I replied defiantly.

Joshua towered over me, placing a hand on the door. I closed my eyes, taking in a deep breath of his scent as he leaned closer, clean with a hint of some manly spice.

I licked my lips, imagining his taste.

"Command me to my knees, Goddess. *Please*," he whispered. "I want to taste you."

As much as I loved the professor on his knees, the fact that he was trying to tell me what to do made me want to do the opposite.

"No," I said, opening my eyes.

Joshua froze, his brow furrowed.

"What do you mean *no*?" He took a step back.

"Just that, no."

Joshua flexed his hands by his sides, balling them into fists and releasing a few times. I learned from our first night in Florida how much he hated the word no. He wasn't the type to force himself, thankfully, but that never stopped him from pouting. *Men.*

"I can't figure you out. I thought you liked it when I knelt for you." The pouting was turning into a mini tantrum as he huffed, throwing his hands in the air.

"I like it when you don't tell me what to do. We've been over this," I replied with an even voice.

I wanted to match his energy, throw my own fit about people trying to control me, but that wouldn't get us anywhere. That, and I didn't want to have a fight without any clothes on.

Joshua's face fell as I pushed past him to grab the towel off the floor. Without a word, I wrapped it around my body and turned toward the bedroom.

"Wait," he said, grabbing my arm. "I-I didn't. I wasn't—fuck!" He ran a hand down his face while letting out a sigh of defeat. "You're right, I'm sorry."

I took the time to gather my thoughts before speaking, keeping an impassive expression on my face. It was times like this that I wish I had more confidence in myself, or more experience with men. I didn't want to push Joshua away, but I needed to make it clear who was in charge.

"I forgive you," I said, breaking the brief silence.

Joshua relaxed, the tension in his body melting away. Knowing that he was just as afraid of losing me made it easier to not stay angry.

"Thank you." His voice was tender, awakening all sorts of warm and fuzzy feelings inside of me.

"Don't thank me yet," I teased, "wait until we discuss your punishment."

"Wait. What?" Joshua called out, but I didn't wait. I was already walking off, knowing he would follow.

Episode 32
Punishment

Joshua

"Cassie, talk to me!" I called out as I followed her into my room.

"I'll be more than happy to discuss your punishment after I'm dressed," she replied without turning around.

Punishment. I wished she wouldn't keep saying that word. It set me on edge. Punishment implied I fucked up big time, and that made me sick to my stomach.

"I'm sorry, Cassie. I don't always think clearly when a beautiful woman is standing in front of me without any clothes on," I pleaded.

She paused in front of my closet, spinning on her heels before marching toward me. Her face twisted in anger as she looked up at me. Fuck, what did I do now?

"How often is that a problem?" she demanded, placing a hand on her hip.

"How often is what a problem?" I asked, feeling exasperated. Couldn't I get one morning where we didn't fight? This was never a problem with Janet. We rarely fought. *And she broke up with you, never explaining why.*

"Having to think clearly with a beautiful woman standing in front of you without any clothes on," she said, throwing my words back at me.

You walked right into that one.

At least I knew why she was upset. I needed to be more mindful of my words when Cassie was like this. In her anger, she missed that I was trying to compliment her. *To get out of your punishment.*

I needed to touch her, to ground myself, before I let my frustrations spiral. Reaching out, I trailed my fingers down her arm, watching her skin pebble in response.

"Only you, which is why I'm out of practice." I held my breath, hoping that stupid line did the trick.

Eddie was the smooth talker. I never needed to spout fancy lines on the fly. On the rare occasions I found myself in a precarious position, he was usually nearby. Not this time, and I definitely would not want him near an undressed Cassie. It would be handy, though.

The frown slowly melted from her lips.

"Smooth talk isn't going to keep you from facing the consequences of your actions. Maybe a little discipline will help you remember," she said with a wink.

Before I could argue further, a loud knock came from the front. Breakfast.

"Hold that thought," I said, turning to head out of the room.

There was no way I would let Cassie bend me over and spank me like a naughty child. It was demeaning, emasculating, and likely the only deal breaker I had at this point. If I put my foot down and made sure she understood it would never happen, she'd back off. She had to

.

After grabbing the food from where it was left in front of the door, I placed it on the kitchen counter and headed back to the bedroom. The whole time, I stewed over my coming *punishment*, planning my argument. I needed to make Cassie see reason.

Back in the bedroom, Cassie sat on my bed wearing one of my shirts, scrolling on her phone. My feet froze in the doorway as I admired how right she looked surrounded by pieces of me. *Walk it back, buddy. Too soon.*

"I'm ordering some necessities to be delivered here. And some cheap spare clothes since I keep forgetting extras." She didn't look up as she spoke.

I hated she wasn't looking at me. It reminded me of how easily she pretended not to notice me on the first day of class. The helpless feeling from that day crept its way under my skin, filling me with doubt.

"Is this my punishment?" I asked, unsure when I became so needy.

Cassie looked up from the glowing screen, her expression pained.

"I'm not trying to take over your space or anything. Sorry if keeping some toiletries here is overreach—"

"No, not that!" *Fuck.* How was I so bad at this? "You didn't look up while talking. I thought maybe you were ignoring me."

"If I was ignoring you, then I wouldn't have said anything, Joshua. You need to relax."

"Yes, relax. So easy when your girlfriend openly says she wants to punish you," I replied dryly.

Cassie looked up from her phone, letting out a sigh.

"On your knees, Professor," she whispered softly, pointing to a spot on the floor next to the bed.

Those words were my lifeline. I eagerly sprang to the spot, dropping to my knees. Her skin felt warm against my cheek as I rested it on her lap, the tension immediately evaporating from my body. Here I was safe. *We* were safe.

"You're looking at the whole punishment thing the wrong way. This is your opportunity to prove you can follow directions," she explained.

Her fingers combed through my hair as she petted me, lulling me into my peaceful place. It was easier to articulate my thoughts without panic fogging my mind.

"I'm not going to let you spank me," I stated calmly.

"Okay? That's random."

That wasn't the response I expected. Doubt trickled in as I pressed further.

"That's not the punishment, either?"

Cassie burst into a fit of laughter. Again, not the response I expected, but I couldn't help feeling relief.

"No. Oh my God, no! Why? Why would you think that?" she asked before bursting into more giggles.

"Because that's what happens in—" I stopped myself before I could say porn. Cassie didn't need to know about my recent *research* into our dynamic.

"In what?" she pressed, raising an eyebrow.

"Never mind. Just tell me already. It's driving me crazy," I said, hoping to veer the conversation anywhere else.

"Your punishment? Or the order I just placed on Amazon?" she asked, smiling.

She was teasing me, and I couldn't help enjoying it. The conversation I dreaded had become fun and lighthearted. The weight of our fight was now miles away.

"Punishment. Please, put me out of my misery." I playfully nipped her thigh.

"No masturbation for one week."

Episode 33
A Needed Conversation

Cassie

"What?" Joshua looked up at me with eyes wide and mouth agape. If he had been one of Grandmother's friends, he would have been clutching his pearls.

"No. Masturbation. For. One. Week," I said slower.

"I heard you. But why?"

Because I want an excuse to tease you. Because I love the rush I feel having that kind of power over you.

"It will inconvenience you enough to get my point across without hurting you. I don't get off on causing you pain. You do know that, right?"

I ran my fingers through his soft hair, trying to soothe him as he stared at me with puppy dog eyes. The vulnerability in his features called to me, begging me to comfort and care for him.

"I know, I just don't understand," he said with a sigh. Joshua was still pouting, like he did whenever I used the word no. *Someone is used to being spoiled.*

"Women always fall at your feet and do anything you want, don't they?" I hadn't meant for it to come out so accusatory, more of an observation, but there was a flash of hurt in Joshua's eyes.

"No... if that was the case, I wouldn't have met you until the first day of class." *Oh... The ex...*

My hands balled into fists in his sheets as I fought to keep a pleasant smile. If Joshua sensed I was upset, he'd assume it was his fault. It was the biggest gaping wound she left behind, and I hated her for it.

He was better off without her, but I wasn't sure if he knew that yet. Someone who ghosts you after a long-term relationship likely never cared. Not that I would ever say that out loud. Joshua had been through enough, and that thought was probably already running through his head without me saying anything.

The professor deserved someone who cared about his happiness. *You care.* I did. I knew what it felt like to be adrift with nothing to ground me. Knowing I could be there for him, it felt like I was helping myself in a way.

"Then you proved things turn out much better when you don't get your way," I said with a smile and a wink. It was a risky move that could easily devolve back into a fight, but I couldn't help teasing him just a little.

Joshua stared daggers at me, but his lips curved upwards. He was a little puppy dog, all bark and no bite.

"Fine. Fine. But can we talk about something else now? Like break-fast. I ordered delivery, and it's sitting in the kitchen, getting cold."

I let Joshua lead me to the kitchen and divvy up the food. I had noticed over the weekend that he looked just as peaceful performing small acts of care as he did on his knees. *He needs to feel useful.*

My heart broke a little with that realization. It likely stemmed from the breakup, as well.

I took a few bites of my food as I mulled over how to ask what I wanted without starting another fight. Between Joshua's baggage and mine, every conversation was a potential minefield. If we didn't try to work through some of it now, then we would keep setting each other off.

"You're quiet," Joshua said, pulling me from my thoughts. His lips were pressed into a thin line as he watched.

And there was my opening.

"It makes you nervous," I pointed out, watching his reaction.

He tensed at the accusation, not even attempting to deny it. His eyes dropped to the omelet on his plate as he started picking at it with his fork. It would be easy to drop it and change the subject, but then things would never get better.

"I know it's because of her, and I'm not mad at you or jealous. I just—" Taking in a breath, I worked through my next words carefully before speaking them out loud. I didn't want Joshua to feel attacked. "You're obviously still hurting, even if you don't want to admit it. Talk me through what happened, what she was like."

"Why?" Joshua asked without looking up from his plate. His expression blanked as if he needed to guard himself around me. It hurt.

Rationally, it made sense. We were barely a thing, and I was asking a lot, but the moments we had shared were pretty intense, giving us the illusion of a deeper connection. Or maybe it wasn't an illusion and things just escalated at a faster pace because of it. In the end, it didn't matter. I just needed answers so I knew how to reassure him.

Reaching out, I traced my fingers along the back of his hand.

"Because I like being your source of comfort. I like it a lot. But I can't do a good job if I don't know what your needs are. Just give me something other than high school sweethearts. Please?"

Silence fell between us as Joshua contemplated my request. I could almost see the war he was waging in his head as he tried to decide whether to say yes or no.

You are the one in charge. Take control.

Joshua needed an anchor when anxious, but I didn't want him on his knees for this conversation. Instead, I rose from my seat and pushed my way into his lap. The tension melted from his body as I wrapped my arms around him, cuddling against his chest.

"Talk to me," I pleaded softly.

Joshua nuzzled the top of my head, planting a soft kiss. "You won't be mad?"

"As long as you're honest, I won't hold anything you say against you." It wasn't quite what he asked, but I didn't want to make a promise I couldn't keep.

"There was a time when I thought we would get married," he confessed. "We were watching a movie one night, a rom-com I don't remember much about. She went off about the proposal and how tacky it was. Personally, I thought it was sweet, but I didn't want an argument. It made me a little gun-shy, like I might ask her wrong and then she'd say no. As time went on, it kept happening. Any time a proposal or wedding came on TV, she would complain and pick it apart. It felt like she knew I wanted to propose and was not so subtly warning me not to."

He grew quiet, so I offered what I hoped were words of comfort.

"I'm sorry. That must have been frustrating."

Way to be generic. I cringed. Having never been in a situation close to what he described, I didn't really know what else to say.

"At first, but then I realized I didn't need a ring or ceremony to be happy with her. For me, just having her in my life was enough. I..." Joshua paused, suddenly wrapping his arms around me. "I thought she felt the same way, too. I mean, we never fought. She never told me she was unhappy. At the time, I would have done anything, but she never told me."

"And now you're worried I will wake up one day and drop you without explanation or a chance to fix things."

"Yes," he whispered. I could hear the heartbreak and fear in his voice. One word shouldn't carry such heavy emotions.

I understood his fear. The truth was that there could have been nothing wrong between them, at least nothing fixable. She might have woken up and decided she wanted to be single. Or maybe he was so focused on her aversion to weddings that he missed other things. In the end, it didn't matter. They were done, and Joshua needed to remember that I wasn't Janet.

"Except I've told you every time you've upset me. And instead of ending things, I correct your behavior," I teased.

Joshua stiffened, pulling back to look at me. Relief washed over his features when he noticed my smile.

"I'm not a dog," he said, scrunching his face.

"No, but you are mine, and I'm not letting you go that easy."

Leaning in, I pressed my lips to his, proving my claim with a tender kiss. Joshua hummed in approval before pulling back and whispering the last thing I expected to hear.

"Spend winter break with me in Florida."

Episode 34

Fears

Joshua

"I'm sorry. I meant that to be a question not an order," I blurted out.

Fuck. Instead of walking the words back, I doubled down with that sad apology. What was wrong with me? My stomach churned as Cassie pulled back to face me. Fear gripped me, forcing my hold on her to tighten. I couldn't risk her moving, I needed my anchor.

Here comes the rejection. I steadied myself, knowing the unwelcome thought was the likely outcome.

"I don't think we are to the point of making long-term plans," she said, her eyes searching mine.

My heart sank. She wasn't wrong, but it was still disappointing. Part of me hoped Cassie was just as swept up in all of this as I was, but that clearly wasn't the case.

"Of course not. It slipped out, sorry," I said, casting my eyes to the floor.

The only thing left was to lick my wounds and move on. It was only a little embarrassment. It could have been worse, and I could have asked her to move in. *At least you aren't that crazy, Joshua.*

"Joshua," Cassie cooed softly as she lifted my chin, "I'm not saying no. Ask me again in a month, okay?" She offered a frail smile as she waited.

"Okay," I said, nodding slowly.

I tried to decipher the meaning behind her words. Did that mean she was saying yes? I couldn't fathom her wanting me to ask again just to tell me no a second time. Cassie wasn't cruel. *Unless you count her punishment.* Even that was tame, all things considered.

The mood between us shifted. My body felt lighter knowing I still had a chance.

"Good," Cassie said with a little clap. "So, now that we've settled that, what are our plans for today? Have you canceled classes yet?"

I couldn't stop the smile tugging at my lips. Cassie seemed completely unbothered from the rollercoaster of obstacles thrown at us this morning. She smiled back at me with unbridled excitement in her eyes.

Cassie wants to spend the day with me. She still wants me. All the stress of the morning disappeared as I let her enthusiasm infect me.

"Who says I'm canceling my afternoon class?" I teased, raising one brow.

My cock stiffened as she wiggled in my lap, leaning closer. Goosebumps trailed over my skin as her soft lips trailed kisses up my neck. This was nice.

A moan slipped out as she reached my ear. The sting of her teeth biting my lobe proved to be more pleasure than pain, judging by my raging hard-on. *Well, that's new.*

"*Me.*" The word was a breathy whisper that sent a shiver of arousal through my veins.

I swallowed around a lump that formed in my throat. My thoughts were blurred, unable to focus on anything other than the young, pants-less blonde sitting in my lap. The heat of her pussy soaked through my pants. *God bless gray sweatpants.*

"Are you wearing underwear?" I managed to choke out. Why those were the words that slipped from my lips instead of something relevant, I couldn't tell you.

"Silly Professor." Cassie giggled, adjusting her position so she straddled me. *Thank you, God.*

I took advantage of the new position, cupping her ass. No, she was not wearing underwear. I let out a groan, my hips thrusting upward with the discovery.

"About classes—" Cassie tried to continue the conversation as if she wasn't purposely distracting me with her body, but I swiftly cut her off.

"I'll send out emails in a bit. I just want to enjoy this a little more. *Please, Cassie,*" I begged, my fingers digging into her flesh.

My sweet Goddess answered with her delicious lips on mine. I gladly granted her entrance, sucking on her tongue as it explored my mouth. Cassie threaded her fingers through my hair, holding firm as her intentions became more aggressive. Every muscle in my body relaxed, eagerly submitting to her desires.

A faint buzzing noise accompanied by a familiar ringtone interrupted the moment. *Dammit.*

"Is that your phone?" Cassie asked, pulling away.

A growl of frustration slipped out at the loss of her kiss-swollen lips.

"It's just Eddie. Ignore it." There was no disguising my annoyance at the distraction.

Leaning in, I tried to continue our make-out session, but Cassie dodged my advances.

"How do you know?"

"He has his own ringtone," I answered, growing increasingly frustrated.

"Answer it," she commanded.

"What? Why?"

"I don't want him turning up uninvited again. You're mine today."

I hated to admit it, but Cassie was right. Eddie had been hovering since my breakup. Knowing my luck, he *would* drive all the way here because I didn't answer my phone.

Tightening my hold around Cassie, I lifted her with me as I stood up. I would not put my Goddess down just because I had to answer the stupid phone. Laughter burst from her as she wrapped her arms and legs around me for support. Once in my bedroom, I placed Cassie on the bed, kissing her again before reaching for the phone.

"Shouldn't you be getting ready for work, or going to work, or at work?"

"That is a shitty way to greet your best friend," Eddie replied.

I let out a sigh, taking a seat next to Cassie on the bed.

"Sorry, man. It's just been an interesting morning. You kind of interrupted breakfast," I explained.

Cassie moved closer, laying her head in my lap as she wrapped her arms around me. What little fight I had left vanished as she cuddled into me.

"Interrupted breakfast? On a school day? Don't you normally do something quick? Or is that code for your little rebound?" I could mentally picture his goofy eyebrow wiggle on the other end of the line as he teased me.

"Yes," I huffed out, hoping he would take the hint.

"Yes what? Wait! Is she there now? Put me on speaker," Eddie ordered excitedly.

I wished he was kidding, but he wasn't.

"I'm not putting you on speaker so you can embarrass us both, Eddie." I should have been happy he was taking a positive interest in Cassie. God knows he never did with Janet.

Without warning, Cassie grabbed the phone right out of my hand. I tried to grab it back, but she held up a finger in warning. I watched helplessly as she put the call on speaker, dreading the chaos that was about to unfold.

"Good friends don't cockblock, Eddie. Unless you get off on listening to your friend having his cock sucked?" My mouth dropped open at her unexpected response, my cheeks burning. Cassie only smiled and winked.

"Hey, kiddo. I didn't know you two were busy, or I wouldn't have bothered the guy. I just wanted to check in," Eddie replied. Of course, *he* was unfazed by the conversation.

"How are things with that girl?" Cassie asked.

It was unsettling how easily the two seemed to converse. I should have been elated that my best friend and my girlfriend were getting along. His inability to even try with Janet had hurt, leaving me to play constant peacemaker. Yet here he was gabbing away with Cassie in a manner that was far too friendly for my liking.

Part of me knew that was just Eddie. He was a salesman at heart, a natural people person, but that didn't stop the jealousy from clawing at me. Cassie was mine, not his. This was *our* time he was intruding on. It wasn't right that their conversation could flow so easily when I struggled.

"Good. Strange. Honestly, I think I need an outside opinion. What are you two doing Saturday night? Can I bring her over for dinner?"

Over the conversation and not thrilled with the direction it was heading, I stepped in. My time with Cassie was precious. If Eddie needed to talk, we could schedule something when she was busy.

"No—"

"Of course," Cassie said. "You are in charge of the food, though."

What just happened?

"Fantastic. I'll let you two get back to whatever it was you were doing. Bye, kiddo."

"Bye Eddie." Cassie then hung up the phone and tossed it on the bed.

I stared at her, blinking a few times as I tried to gather my thoughts.

"You can't do that," I blurted out.

Cassie sat up, cocking her head to the side. "Do what?"

The innocent look she gave me wasn't fooling anyone. Yes, she was beautiful, staring at me all doe-eyed while she bit her bottom lip. Yes, it was distracting me with thoughts of her biting me some more, but I would not let what she did go.

"Make plans for us without consulting me! That's a definite over-step."

To my frustration, Cassie didn't match my energy. She sat calmly beside me, refusing to engage in a fight.

"On your knees, Professor." The words slipped from her lips like a song.

Instead of obeying, I pushed back. "Now's not the time. I want to talk about this."

"Knees, *now*," she snapped.

The firm tone triggered something inside me. Before my mind could process the command, I was kneeling next to the bed.

"Good boy. Now, take a deep breath." Her hands combed through my hair as I begrudgingly filled my lungs.

"You're being condescending," I pouted after a long exhale.

"No, I'm calming you down so we can talk."

Cassie scooted to the edge of the bed, hanging her legs off the side. I took the opportunity to lay my head in her lap, closing my eyes as she continued to pet me. The fight drained out of me as she lulled me into a tranquil headspace.

"You should have let me handle him."

She didn't acknowledge my statement, waiting a beat before speaking.

"When would you have scheduled a time to hang out with him?" Silence. Cassie let out a sigh. "You weren't going to."

She wasn't wrong. I wasn't in the mood for his behavior lately and all the smothering. I needed space. *We* needed space.

"He's worse with boundaries than you are," I teased.

"Then you need to talk to him about it, not avoid him. Unless... are you hoping to end the friendship?"

End... the friendship?

Her question sent a bolt of panic through me. I sat up, taking a few deep breaths to settle the unease at her suggestion. No, Eddie was my best friend. All I wanted was a little space, nothing as drastic as ending the friendship.

"I just want space," I whispered to myself.

"Then, tell him on Saturday. He'll be more likely to listen once he sees you're okay."

I didn't bother asking her to explain what she meant. It wouldn't make a difference in the grand scheme of things. Instead, I laid my head back in her lap and took the time to recenter myself.

Episode 35

Confrontations and Accountability

Cassie

Some random show streamed on the TV while we sat on the couch, Joshua's head in my lap. Despite the intimacy of our position, I couldn't help feeling like there was still an invisible wall dividing us. I thought things would have calmed down after he left briefly to retrieve his car, but the cloud that had haunted us most of the morning was still looming.

"If you don't like the show, we can change it," Joshua said, interrupting my thoughts. He looked up at me, eyes full of concern.

"Huh? No, it's fine," I lied.

"You're frowning pretty intently, Cassie. I really don't mind if we put on something else."

My poor professor. Even when he's mad at me, he wants to please me. His need to put me first made me wonder if it was less about his breakup and just who he was as a person. It would explain so much. Still, I wasn't ready to have a full conversation about the weird vibe in the air, not until I was sure I had a grasp on why.

"Sorry. I was lost in thought," I confessed, hoping he would lose interest and drop it.

Joshua sat up, his brow lined with worry.

"What are you thinking about that has you so upset?" There was no mistaking the tightness in his voice or the way he held his breath. *Great, you've gone and panicked him, Cassie.*

"Nothing," I tried to protest, but the look he gave me said he wasn't buying it. This conversation was happening whether or not I wanted it to, apparently. "Fine. You're mad at me. And don't say you're not because you totally are."

My breaths were heavy as I stared him in the eyes, but my chest felt lighter. The professor seemed to relax as well. The tightness in his posture melted away as he leaned back on the couch.

"You snatched my phone, made plans for the both of us without consulting me, and never apologized." His expression was indifferent, like he didn't just call me out point-blank.

"I...I..." My cheeks burned as I stumbled for something to say. When he put it like that, I sounded like a bitch. "I'm sorry. I wasn't trying—"

"I know you weren't, but it was still disrespectful." He was coddling me, despite the firmness of his words. I could hear it in his voice, the gentle tone to comfort me while simultaneously reprimanding me. Why did it make me feel worse?

I dipped my head, avoiding eye contact as I mulled over what he said. *Disrespectful.* My shoulders slumped as reality set in. My attempts to be helpful were anything but. I was a bully.

"Hey, look at me," Joshua said softly as he lifted my chin. "I get it. This is new... weird, and we are just trying to figure it out. I just don't get the luxury of doling out punishments when my boundaries are violated."

Excuse me? There was far too much to unpack in that bomb of a statement. I tensed, clenching my fist as I grasped for the right words to convey the wide range of emotions warring inside of me. No, I shouldn't have taken his phone, and maybe I should have been softer after, but the punishment was necessary to enforce a line he had crossed a few times. Right?

The longer I worked through it, the tighter my chest felt. Each breath became shallower as my heart pounded inside my chest. I felt like a stupid child. Hell, that's probably how I looked to the professor. Just a dumb student like all the others.

Joshua's lips pressed into mine, pulling my mind from the swirling tempest that threatened to unravel me. I melted under his tender affections, letting the anger and panic drain away.

"I'm teasing," he whispered against my lips.

"No, you're not."

"No, I'm not," he agreed with a smile, resting his head against mine.

At least one of us is in a better mood, I thought bitterly. Guilt followed as I cursed myself. Of course I wanted him in a better mood. That's how this whole mess started. As embarrassing as all of this was, I needed to put on my big girl panties and suck it up.

"I really am sorry," I said with a sigh.

"I know," Joshua replied as he pulled me into his lap and wrapped his arms around me. "We'll get there at some point. Together."

I hung my key to the apartment on the hook next to the door as I entered. Next, I grabbed my phone and sent the professor a quick text letting him know I made it home okay. He seemed genuinely upset with himself over not being able to drive me home, but we both agreed that was a risk we weren't willing to take yet. Within seconds, the phone buzzed with his reply.

Good Boy: Glad the bus didn't take too long. I miss you already.

"Look at you, all smiles!" Nicole sauntered over, nudging me with her shoulder when she drew near. "I'd say you missed a fun time last night, but I have a feeling you and your secret older man made your own fun. Is he already sending you dirty messages?"

"There were some fun parts," I said with a tired smile.

After we talked things through again, the dark cloud that had been haunting us lifted and we were able to enjoy ourselves. We had lunch delivered, and then I enjoyed a few orgasms as the professor had me for dessert. All in all, a lovely and relaxing day... except that I never really got over the events of the morning. I hid it well, but I second-guessed every interaction for the rest of the day, worried I would take things too far again. It was nice to be home where I could decompress and work through things without having to worry about Joshua's reaction.

I must have been standing, lost in my thoughts, for a while because Nicole had a frown on her face.

"What?" I finally asked after one too many seconds of silence passed by.

Nicole shrugged as she shook her head.

"I dunno. I thought you would look more wrecked, and not in the solemn way. Isn't that the point of dating an older man? Crazy sex with a guy that knows what he is doing."

Was it?

With a heavy sigh, I dropped my purse on the floor with a thud and headed to the living room with Nicole hot on my heels. I had no idea how to respond to her question. The allure of Professor Grant wasn't that he was older, though I found his *mature* appearance incredibly hot. I liked that he let me be the one in control, and that he needed me in order to feel safe and grounded. But I had no idea what I was doing and almost messed it all up.

That was the problem—my inexperience. After the mishap today, it was clear I was in over my head. Honestly, I was surprised that the professor was as chill about everything as he was. *It's because he's still broken from his ex. Once he has his confidence back, he'll find someone who knows what they're doing.* The thought of him moving on made my stomach twist in knots, a reaction far too intense for a relationship as new as ours.

Slumping on the couch, I let out another sigh as I looked up at my friend with big, puppy dog eyes.

"I'm in over my head, Nicole. I don't know how to be a Domme!"

Her eyes widened as her jaw dropped to the floor.

"A Domme? What the fuck, Cassie!"

"That came out wrong. Ugh! Where do I start?" I dropped my head into my hands and let out a noise of frustration.

The couch dipped as Nicole took a seat next to me, placing a supportive hand on my shoulder.

"Why don't you start at the beginning?"

The beginning. I could do that.

"I told you before that he lets me be in control a lot of the time." I looked at my friend as she nodded. "I've noticed that when I give him commands anytime he's stressed, it levels him out a little. Usually, it leads to something sexy or even a bit intimate. And I love the power I feel from it."

"I could see where that would give someone a bit of a high," Nicole admitted.

"Right? Except today something happened, and I thought I was being helpful like usual, but I crossed a line, and he got mad and now I... I just feel like an idiot."

The room fell silent as the seconds ticked by. I thought talking about it would help release some of the pressure that had been building, but my chest still felt tight and the knot in my stomach grew larger. Talking wasn't helping. I needed solutions.

"Is he even looking for a Domme or just a little soft roleplay in the bedroom?" Nicole finally asked.

"Wh-what?" I stared at my friend, dumbfounded.

"Does he want a Domme or a little power play?"

Nicole spoke calmly, like this was an everyday kind of conversation between us. Where was the shock and outrage from a few moments ago?

"I—I'm not sure. Probably somewhere in between, based on what we've talked about," I answered, trying to match her energy. Not that I was succeeding in the least. I could feel the burn of my flushed cheeks, and my hands wouldn't stay still as I twisted my fingers together.

"Okay, so you two have talked about it."

"A little. Neither one of us really knows what we are doing. We've established I like being in control, and he likes taking orders, and we've put limits on some of the places we can play," I explained, leaving out that the college was one of those places. *And you still fuck around there, despite agreeing not to.* Shut up, brain.

"That's something. Do you have safe words?" I shook my head. "Okay...that might be part of the problem. Have you discussed likes and dislikes outside of the power dynamic?" I shook my head again.

Instead of feeling better, the conversation was making me feel worse. Sure, I've heard about safe words. Who hasn't? I just always assumed they were for people doing hardcore stuff not messing around like us. As for the likes and dislikes, I had no excuse. I never needed to have that kind of conversation before. *Because you were always too eager to please the guy before.* That, and their requests were usually pretty vanilla. The only conversation we've had past our power dynamic that I could remember was this morning when he complained about being punished.

"Wait! He mentioned being punished stresses him out. He hates feeling like he failed me." A new wave of guilt washed over me as I started second-guessing how I handled that conversation, too.

"Okay, that's something. Sounds like he has a praise kink. Maybe look into Soft Dommes and see if that would be something you both like."

"Soft... Domme?" *There are different kinds?* I blinked a few times as my brain tried to process this new information. I assumed whatever we were doing didn't really exist, or it wasn't really BDSM, or something like that. Here Nicole was, calling it by name, like it was no big deal and everyone should know about it. *Should have looked harder when browsing online.* Apparently.

"How do you even know what that is?" I asked. Nicole was my BFF. We told each other everything. How did I not know she was so versed in this stuff? *How does she not know you're fucking your professor?*

"We aren't talking about me, Cassie. We are talking about *you* and your mystery older boyfriend with a praise kink. I think if you do a little research on that topic, it might help you plan a more detailed conversation about needs and boundaries. If you're going to get into kink, then you need to do some real research, babe."

"You're right," I conceded, "think you can help me?"

A big smile stretched across Nicole's face. "Of course. It sounds like a lot more fun than what I had planned."

Episode 36
The Waiting Game

Joshua

My phone sat on my desk, mocking me with its lack of notifications. I was supposed to be reading assignments and making my preliminary notes, but the damn phone wouldn't let me. I tried to put it in my desk drawer, but then I kept opening it to check and see if I missed a text or call. Both Cassie and Eddie had gone strangely silent since Wednesday. I was able to convince myself yesterday that, between classes and assignments, Cassie was just busy, but now it was Friday, and I still hadn't heard from her. Not a good morning, good night, not even the daily lingerie pictures she had been sending.

My fingers itched to text her, tell her I missed her, but I couldn't bring myself to do it. What if I came across as needy? No, she would reach out when she wanted to talk. *Unless she's waiting for you to text her.* That stray thought had been plaguing me since the night before. The last message in our chat log was when I acknowledged she made it home safe. I stared at it often over the last two days, wondering if that message was the reason I hadn't heard from her. The fear of coming off needy stopped me every time I started to type something out.

You'll see her Saturday. Will I? And even if I did, Eddie would be there too. Not that I wasn't looking forward to seeing him, but...

While the silence from Cassie was crippling me, I enjoyed Eddie was no longer trying to run my life. I didn't hate my friend, but his sudden need to be up my ass after my breakup was suffocating. Now that I had space to breathe, I didn't dread the thought of hanging out... I just wish it wasn't time that was meant for Cassie and me.

Amusingly enough, the only person I had heard from over the past two days was the new history professor. Zach texted early Thursday to smooth over any perceived awkwardness from his drunken flirtations, which developed into a casual exchange throughout the day. Despite being so young, I liked the guy. While definitely a little green, he was genuine. *And he doesn't try to plan out every free second of your life.*

I let out a long sigh, leaning back in my chair to stretch. The day had barely begun, and it was already dragging. There was no way I would make it through the end of the day.

Should have stayed home. I shook the thought from my head. Working from home would have been worse. I only came in because my office was a more productive environment for working. *No, you were hoping to run into Cassie on campus.*

"Knock, knock," Zack called out as he opened the door to my office, saving me from the spiral I was about to fall into.

He took a few steps in, a sheepish look on his face as he spotted the stack of papers on my desk. Call me old-fashioned, but I found it easier to print them out and go through each one with a red pen. Was it more work in the long run? Probably, but old habits die hard.

"I'm not interrupting anything, am I? If you're busy, I can come back later."

"No, I'm not busy," I said as I waved him in. *Just kicking myself for not having a copy of Cassie's schedule.*

His face lit up as he approached my desk and took a seat.

"Great! Fantastic! I was hoping you would be free."

I held back a smirk from his enthusiasm. Zack may dress himself professionally—collared button-down shirt, nice pants, and a tie—but it did little to hide his youthfulness. If he dressed more casually, like I often did, he would likely be mistaken for a student. His excited energy only exacerbated things.

"What's up? More problems with the student body?" I asked.

In a college setting, fresh meat wasn't usually an issue. The students were older and more mature than their high school counterparts. It helped that none of them were forced to attend classes. Everyone was here because they wanted to learn. Those who didn't would drop out instead of causing a scene.

Unfortunately, we faced a different set of problems. Most of the students who hit on me didn't understand why sleeping with a student was inappropriate, or maybe they didn't care. I had heard the phrase *"but we are both consenting adults"* more times than I cared to count. *And not once in those situations would I have been consenting.*

"No. I mean, yes, but that's not why I'm here," he replied, looking a bit flushed. *That's not a concerning response at all...*

"Everything okay?" I pressed, leaning forward.

"Maybe?" He shrugged with a tilt of his head. The look of uncertainty was both comical and concerning.

An awkward silence fell over the room as Zack collected his thoughts. The man was quite animated, his facial expressions exaggerated as he held what I could only assume was an entire conversation in his head. I let it drag on for a few more seconds before clearing my throat to remind him I was in the room.

"Sorry! Are you free tonight? Not for a date. I mean, it might be a date, or I thought it was a date, but then I found out his friends will be there. Or maybe they're his coworkers? I wasn't clear on that part."

I listened to Zack ramble on with an amused look on my face. With as easy as it was to rile him up, it was no wonder the students were coming on so strong. They were likely feeding off his over-the-top reactions.

"Hold up," I said when he finally paused for air. "Let's rewind and take it from the top. Who are you going on a maybe date with?"

"This guy I met on a dating app. Since I'm new to the area as a whole, I signed up to meet people. There is this guy on there that I have been chatting with. He lives in the city. We had plans tonight," he explained, much calmer this time.

"And his friends-slash-coworkers will be there?"

"Yeah, something like that." He nodded as he nervously wiped his hands on his pants. "I don't think that was the original plan, but after Tuesday night—"

"You were with me Tuesday night." I definitely don't remember there being a third person.

"I didn't go home with you," Zack countered. A sly smile crossed his lips, the first sign of confidence since he entered my office.

"What did you do when you got home?"

"I drunk dialed him," he confessed. "It was so dumb, but I was feeling..." Zack's face went beet red as he cleared his throat. "You know what? That's not important."

I raised an eyebrow, easily reading between the lines. *He wasn't the only one feeling frisky when he got home.* Yes, but I wasn't about to share that with him. The fewer people who knew about Cassie the better. For now, at least.

"So you called him while drunk," I said, urging him to continue.

"And I barely remember what I said. I think it was mostly dirty talk, but then why would our date become a group thing if that's all that happened?"

"I don't know. You should probably ask him." I shrugged.

"Yeah..."

Zack's shoulders slumped, making me immediately regret my unhelpful response. I knew all too well what it was like to second-guess everything in a budding relationship.

"Sorry. I'm not nearly as wise with relationships as I am with avoiding student advances," I joked. "Why do you want me to come along, anyway? It sounds like your date already has too many people."

"So I'm not completely outnumbered. He's going to be surrounded by people he knows, and I won't. But if you come, I'll know at least one other person."

There was a hopeful look in his eye I couldn't figure out. He couldn't really be asking me to crash his already crowded date. That seemed counterproductive. He needed fewer people, not more.

"Are you sure you want *me*? I'm forty, and you're what? Late twenties, at least, if you are teaching here, but I doubt you're much older. Dragging me out with you, are you sure I won't cramp your style?" I asked, offering him an out.

Zack laughed.

"You make it sound like you're an old man. If you don't want to go, just say so."

"It's not that."

"Then you'll go?"

May as well. Not like you have any plans besides staring at your phone.

"Sure."

"Fantastic!" He leapt from his seat. "I'll text you the details. And I can't thank you enough!"

Like an excited puppy, he bounced with each step as he left my office, shutting the door behind him. *Okay then.* With the click of the door, I let out a breath. *That was different.* Different, but good. Eddie would be proud that I wasn't staying in on a Friday night, if nothing else.

Begrudgingly, I turned my attention back to the stack of papers on my desk. I couldn't put them off any longer if I was going out tonight. *Fun.* Rubbing my eyes, I picked one up and started to read when the rattle of my door opening distracted me.

"Need something else—" The question died in my throat when I saw it wasn't Zack this time. "Cassie?"

"Do you have a minute?"

Episode 37

The Apology Part One

Cassie

"My office hours are on Tuesdays and Thursdays, Miss Jones. You are welcome to schedule a time via email if you need to meet about class." Professor Grant sat straight in his chair, his eyes narrowed in my direction. There wasn't a hint of the soft familiarity I was used to when he spoke.

Oh, he's mad. Of course he was mad. We'd discussed boundaries on campus, and here I was crossing them again even if it was for a greater purpose.

Watching him play the role of stern professor amused me more than it should have. While more confident in the classroom, his demeanor was always friendly and relaxed. This was a new side to the professor, one that I shouldn't push too far. I took another step into his office, leaning my back against the door as I closed it. The urge to run from his icy glare was strong, but I pushed ahead. *Can't fix anything if we don't talk*, I told myself. Though standing here, I wondered if I actually knew what needed fixing.

"This isn't about class, *Professor*. It's a personal matter, if you have the time."

Professor Grant stared at me with an unreadable expression. Pulling my bottom lip between my teeth, I stared back, suddenly unsure. Maybe coming here was a mistake after all. Maybe I should have waited for Saturday—

No, backing down was not an option. I spent the entire walk here psyching myself up to do this. Waiting wouldn't make things easier, and we'd have an audience then. It needed to be now.

"Now is not the time or place, *Miss Jones*," he said in an icy tone before returning his attention to the papers on his desk. I was being...dismissed. *Oh, hell fucking no!*

My vision went red as my hands balled into tight fists at my sides. How dare he dismiss me after all the time I've spent researching things and forming a plan! Scouring the internet for niche BDSM communities was not something I did for fun. The number of things I stumbled upon yesterday that couldn't be unseen—

The sting of my nails digging into my palm brought me back to reality. The professor had no idea what I've been up to since I got home Wednesday. That's why I was here, to tell him. We couldn't have that conversation if things escalated into an argument.

"I just need a moment, please. It's not a conversation I'm comfortable having in front of your friends tomorrow," I pleaded, hoping he'd back down.

"Then you shouldn't have invited them," he countered without looking up. *Ouch.*

Part of me knew I deserved that, but that didn't make it sting any less. After learning more about Soft Dommes, scenes, and boundaries, I realized pretty quickly I crossed a line inviting Eddie and the mystery girl over. I crossed a few lines lately, if I was being completely honest. But he made it seem like we were okay when I last saw him. Where was this attitude coming from? If he was still this mad, he should have said something sooner.

"I know!" I said, stomping my foot in frustration, fists clenched tightly at my sides. "That's part of why I'm here! Stop being difficult when I'm trying to apologize!"

The professor propped his elbows on his desk, kneading his temples with eyes shut like he was trying to stave off a headache. *Get it together, Cassie! You're making it worse.*

"Stop throwing a tantrum in my—wait. Did you say apologize?" Joshua lifted his head, meeting my gaze with a confused expression. *What is going on with him?*

"Yes. I wanted to apologize, among other things. Is that okay?" I snapped.

He let out a sigh, motioning to the chair in front of his desk.

"You really like to assert yourself, don't you?"

My steps faltered at the accusation as I walked over and took a seat. *You did it again, Cassie.*

"I'm sorry." I couldn't bring myself to look at him, focusing instead on my hand in my lap. "I was so excited to see you and tell you what I learned. I assumed you'd be excited to see me, too."

"You confuse the hell out of me, Cassie. I haven't heard from you since Wednesday, and then you come to my office out of the blue like you haven't been giving me the silent treatment," he said with a twinge of defeat.

The silent treatment? Did he really think one day without a text was the silent treatment? I raised my head, ready to argue how ridiculous he was being, but stopped when I saw the exhaustion on his face. He was serious. A little over twenty-four hours without communication, and he'd convinced himself I was angry or something. Somewhere in the back of my mind alarm bells rang, but I brushed them off. Clinginess was the least problematic thing about our relationship.

"I haven't been giving you the silent treatment. I've been busy between classes and researching...*things.*"

"*Things?*" he repeated with one brow raised. "That doesn't sound suspicious. What about the pictures you usually send every morning? You haven't sent any the last two days."

"The lingerie pictures? I thought it would be a dick move to send sexy pictures when I made a big deal about you not jacking off, especially after everything you said about punishment. It felt like pouring salt on the wound."

"Oh... Yeah, that makes sense," he said sheepishly, sinking back in his chair.

"Actually, your punishment is part of why I am here."

Joshua's posture went stiff. "You said you came to apologize."

"I did," I tried to reassure him, "among other things. It's all connected. Just let me talk before you freak out again."

He took a moment to ponder my request before waving his hand for me to continue. The nerves from my walk over were creeping back over me, making me doubt myself. *You got this, Cassie. Just be confident.*

"First, I want to apologize for not hearing you. You've told me in many different ways what your boundaries are, but I was so concerned with my own that I never really listened to what you were saying. Part of the problem was that I kept trying to put our... dynamic, I guess, into a box even though we already acknowledged it wasn't exactly traditional. I thought I had to be forceful to get you to listen to me because that is how I assumed all relationships like this worked. I didn't listen to your cues or words, and I'm sorry."

Taking a pause to breathe, I studied the professor for a reaction. He seemed unsure, waiting for me to say more. *Kinda hoping he would say all is forgiven.* When I realized he wasn't ready to comment yet, I continued.

"Anyway, I mentioned your punishment. Consider it over. I realize now that's not what you need, and I crossed a line that you asked me not to."

All the tension melted away as Joshua let out a sigh of relief. "Thank you for listening, but what made you change your mind?"

I perked up, excited that he gave me the lead in I needed to discuss the next topic.

"My friend Nicole. When I told her about our fight, she said some things that made me realize I was handling everything all wrong. That's why I've been busy. I've been researching," I said excitedly.

Joshua's face fell. "You told your friend?"

"She still doesn't know about you," I reassured him. "I refer to you as my secret, older boyfriend. She knows not to ask more."

"Okay..." It was clear the professor was skeptical, but I didn't want our conversation to get derailed.

"Don't worry, it's fine. She was actually super helpful and suggested I look up things like Soft Domme and Gentle Domme. After searching through a few websites, it really sounds like something you would be into. That's what I wanted to talk about."

"Soft Domme?" he said with a frown, like the words tasted bitter in his mouth.

"Yes, the focus is more on praise and rewarding good behavior. Very little emphasis on punishment, more of a focus on reassurance and care. I'd be happy to send you some of the links I found so you can look them over and tell me what you think," I said with a big smile on my face. It felt good to talk about everything out loud after going over it all in my head a hundred times.

"I'm not sure, Cassie. I don't know why we need to put labels on what we are doing."

I tried not to let the disappointment of his opposition show. Before Wednesday, I totally agreed that labels were unnecessary, but now I thought they were helpful if for no other reason than it gave me a jumping off point. Having a title helped me find guides and rules that I didn't know we needed until I read them. If I was going to get the professor on board, then I needed to show him how these labels would benefit him, too.

Episode 38
The Apology Part Two

Joshua

I didn't miss the hint of a frown on Cassie's lips before she caught herself. It wasn't labels that bothered me, but rather what she was trying to label. I enjoyed thinking of us as being in a relationship. I called Cassie my girlfriend in my head, despite it feeling a tad juvenile at forty. There was something with the words "Domme" and "sub," though, that made me uneasy. It conjured images of men licking stilettos and being spanked while wearing a dog collar, none of which I found appealing. Tacking the words "soft" or "gentle" at the front didn't change anything in my head. I needed to find the words to properly explain my objections without leading into questions I didn't want to answer.

My thoughts wandered as Cassie rose from her seat, gliding toward me like the Goddess she was. I should have pushed her to stay on the other side of the desk and keep up appearances, but the suggestion died in my throat. The need to feel connected to my Goddess outweighed any self-preservation. I needed my anchor to calm the storms of self-doubt that had been brewing inside me.

"I think you'll understand better if I show you what I mean instead of trying to explain it," she said with a mischievous smile.

"Show me?" My eyes roamed her body with the hunger I had been trying to control since she walked into the room. I should have been wary and continued acting coldly, but my hands itched to pull her closer. I was weak, but at that moment, I couldn't care less. She was here. She was with me.

Cassie nudged my legs apart, dropping to her knees between them. I cursed the khakis I wore as she ran her hands up my thighs, desperately wishing to feel her skin on mine. My eyes fell shut and a thrill of pleasure ran through me when her hand grazed my swelling cock covered by my pants.

"Have you...touched yourself since I left your place Wednesday?"

"No," I answered, barely above a whisper.

As dumb as the so-called punishment was, I couldn't bring myself to disappoint Cassie. Her lack of communication heightened the need for her approval. Part of me feared she'd know if I disobeyed, making things worse between us. Obedience was the right decision. The fact that Cassie was on her knees, coaxing my length to fullness with her delicate touch was proof. If I obeyed, I would be rewarded. The concept was perfectly simple.

My head dropped back, a sigh escaping as Cassie continued to palm my cock through my pants. All the tension melted away as I drifted into blissful oblivion.

"Such a good boy for putting up with my mean punishment." Cassie's soft praise washed over me. "I think you deserve a reward."

Great minds think alike.

Through hooded eyes, I watched as she unfastened my pants and pulled out my cock. It looked perfect in her grasp, leaking precum in anticipation. Cassie's eyes locked with mine as she slowly leaned in and licked the tip clean like she would an ice cream cone. It was a power move, asserting her control despite being the one on her knees, just like that night at the bowling alley. The confidence she displayed was almost enough to make me blow my load all over her face. What a beautiful mess it would be.

And how would you clean it after?

The little voice in the back of my head screamed in warning at how foolish we were being. If someone caught us in our current position, there would be no way to spin it as anything other than what it was. Not a single excuse could explain away a student on her knees with my raging hard on in her hands.

Best-case scenario, I would take the fall entirely. Considering the unlikeliness of walking away with a job, I would at least ensure Cassie didn't get expelled. *Or you could stand your ground about boundaries on campus.* That would be the better solution, but it was impossible to enforce. The only reason I stood my ground earlier was out of anger. Without it to solidify my resolve, I was helpless to her whims.

"Out of your head, Professor," she commanded softly.

Fuck. For not knowing me very long, Cassie was far too good at reading me. Eddie was the only other person who could see into my mind and know when the anxiety was winning.

"When I'm on my knees for you, I expect you to give me your full attention. Understand?"

I didn't think I could get any harder, but there was something about the warmth in her voice mixed with the strict tone of her words that my dick craved. It was like my catnip.

"Yes, my Goddess—oooooh, fuck!" My mind blanked as her lips wrapped around me, sucking me into sweet submission. I sank into my chair, bones turning to jelly as my sweet Goddess bestowed my reward for obeying the rules of her ridiculous punishment. If this was my reward, I would gladly comply with every silly request she threw at me.

Her tongue felt like magic as it stroked my length while she simultaneously sucked, leading me closer and closer to the edge of sweet oblivion. My fingers dug into the armrest as I tried to make the moment last a little longer, but it was a useless endeavor. She wanted me to come; it was evident by the way she worked my cock, and my body was eager to obey.

My vision went white, a string of curses falling from my lips as I exploded in Cassie's mouth. The pleasure rolled over me in waves as I momentarily lost my ability to breathe. Cassie continued to suck me off until she drained me of every last drop and my body went slack once more. My mind fogged over. Any thought past satisfaction became too complicated to process while drunk on the post-orgasmic high. All I could do was grin like an idiot as she stood, wiping the corner of her mouth with her thumb.

"Rewards are better than punishment," she mused in a singsong voice as she tucked me back into my pants.

I responded with some unintelligible sound of contentment that drew a smile on her lips. Words were too difficult and completely overrated.

"I'll text you some links I want you to read before tomorrow night." When I didn't immediately acknowledge the command, she followed up with, "There will be more *rewards* if you do."

"Or you could stay and tell me more now," I offered as I reached out to pull her into my lap. I wanted my Goddess closer, cuddled in my lap while I basked in the glow she created. To my dismay, Cassie took a few steps back, just out of reach.

"I have to get to my next class. And shouldn't you be working?" Her gentle teasing brought me crashing back to reality.

"Fuck. Yes, I do. And we need to stop being so reckless. I'm not the only one that could get in trouble."

Cassie straightened, jarred by my response. Internally, I cursed myself for saying anything that would steal the smile from her face.

"Sorry. I was excited, and I didn't want to apologize via text." The joy left her voice as doubt creeped in. *Good one, Joshua.*

"That's not—that came out wrong. It's not all on you. I need to be more firm—" I tried to reassure her, but Cassie cut me off shaking her head.

"No, it *is* on me. Just read the links when I send them, okay?"

"Um, okay?"

"Promise me," she insisted.

"If it means that much to you, of course." As much as I hated to admit it, I would do pretty much anything she'd ask of me. Cassie was my weakness. The warmth that filled me when her smile returned only confirmed it. At some point, I would have to come to terms with how deep I was with her and how stupid it was, but not today.

"Thank you! I'll send them after my class!"

And then my perky Goddess bounced with happiness, giving me a lovely view as she departed.

Episode 39

Six is a Crowd

Joshua

The brisk night air felt refreshing as I stood outside the door to the Players Arcade and Bar waiting for Zack. The electronic chirps, beeps, and other sounds I couldn't identify poured out into the night, barely muffled by the large glass doors guarding the entrance. I wasn't much of a gamer, unless you counted pinball, which left me wondering what I had gotten myself into.

"Joshua!" Zack called out as he approached.

Waving back with a smile, I took notice of my new friend's appearance. Fitted jeans and a button-up shirt with the sleeves rolled up wasn't a bad date outfit except it felt a little formal for an arcade. *Or maybe you are underdressed in jeans and a t-shirt...* Only if I was the one on a first date.

"Thanks for this, seriously," he said, giving me an awkward pat on the shoulder.

"No worries. Didn't realize you were a gamer," I said, nodding toward the building next to us.

Zack's excited smile faltered as unease settled about him.

"I'm not," he admitted, staring down at the ground while rubbing the back of his head, "Nixon is. He chose this place, kept talking about how fun it was."

Tilting my head, I arched a brow and smirked. "You didn't think a date should be on more neutral territory? Like getting beers somewhere...normal?"

Zack laughed, but it didn't reach his eyes. The poor guy was painfully nervous.

"Honestly? I'm not really up on these things. My idea of a good time is binging obscure history documentaries on YouTube. The only parties I've been to are the ones my college girlfriend dragged me to. I figured if this guy has a place he likes, why not try it out."

I nodded along as he spoke, offering a shrug at his explanation. It hurt to admit it, but I understood him all too well. Not about the obscure history documentaries thing, but the not going out part of it. While I usually ended up enjoying myself, I rarely went out of my own accord. It was always because Eddie, Janet, or someone else invited me out.

"Well, let's get this show on the road," I said.

Zack flashed me a smile before opening the door. "Age before beauty."

I shot him a look, then we both broke into laughter. Zack, while a little awkward, was fun. I liked him. And while this arcade bar was not my usual scene, I didn't mind tagging along to help him out.

Inside was not much louder than outside, to my relief. The ambience of the place was definitely unique, though. While front corner looked like a more traditional bar, while the rest of the venue looked like a teenager decorated it. The copious amount of arcade games with their flashing lights were expected, but the neon 90s decor threw me for a loop. It felt like I stepped into a time machine.

"There they are," Zack said, tugging on my sleeve.

I looked over to where he was pointing, spotting a guy with glasses waving at us enthusiastically from a table in the bar area. He wore a graphic tee with some artsy design on the front and his arms were covered in colorful ink. *Two full tattoo sleeves.* It was honestly a little shocking because the thirty-something, inked up, nerdy, hipster-looking guy was not what I expected Zack to be into.

As we walked over to the table, I took a mental inventory of the woman who sat next to Zack's date with a slightly sour look on her face. While her overall appearance was more subdued than Glasses, the dark bubblegum pink streaks mixed among the chestnut locks of her hair were definitely a statement. *Don't be judgmental.* Moving my attention from Miss Pink, I almost stumbled in surprise when I noticed the other two sitting at the table staring back at me with equally confused expressions.

"What the hell are you doing here?" Eddie asked as I approached the table. "I thought you would be busy with someone else on a Friday night."

Oh, this wasn't good. Zack couldn't know about Cassie. Even if by some miracle he didn't report me, I would be dragging him into the secrecy and scandal if I ever got caught.

I shot Eddie a quick warning, hoping my oldest friend would understand to shut his mouth. He seemed to get the memo, turning to Carla and not so quietly whispering, "Like his right hand."

Nice save, idiot. Still, it was something, though Carla looked less than impressed by the joke.

"Hey, Eddie. Carla. Zack teaches at the college, too. He invited me along since this is apparently a group outing."

Zack looked at Eddie and then back at me as if he was processing everything slowly.

"Wait, Eddie as in the guy that burst into your apartment while naked?"

Internally, I groaned as the table experienced mixed reactions. Miss Pink covered her mouth while she did a spit take that would make even the most skilled comedic actor jealous. Carla gave Eddie a look that said she had questions, a lot of them, while Eddie looked at Zack and me, rather annoyed.

"Hold up! Were you naked bursting in on him, or was he naked when you burst in?" Zack's date—Nixon, I think—asked. He didn't look amused or confused, but genuinely interested. *That's not a weird reaction.*

"He was the naked one, Nixon!" Eddie snapped and then grumbled, "Why would *I* be naked? That doesn't make any sense."

"Neither does using your *emergency key* to my place when there isn't an emergency," I replied.

"Heh, small world," Zack cut in, easing a little of the tension at the table.

He let out a small sigh, shooting his date an apologetic look. Nixon looked completely unfazed by the scene unfolding, grabbing Zack's hand and pulling him closer to whisper something in his ear. I couldn't hear what was being said, but judging by how red Zack turned, I don't think I wanted to know.

Not wanting to intrude on what was likely an intimate moment, I turned my attention back to my friends.

"This doesn't really seem like your kind of place," I said to Eddie.

"I could say the same to you," he replied. I didn't miss the edge in his voice or the way he was glaring at me. *Because you embarrassed him!* No, he embarrassed himself. I'm allowed to discuss one of my best friends violating my privacy with whomever I want. This was just the consequences of his actions.

Carla gave Eddie a swat on the arm, and then pulled up a chair from another table, placing it between her and Miss Pink.

"Here. Sit between Poppy and me. Then you won't have to stare at Eddie while he pouts," she instructed.

Miss Pink, Poppy, smirked, clearly amused by our little exchange. I wasn't in the mood to sit next to such an animated stranger, but there also weren't any other seats. *Just go with it. For Zack.*

"I'm going to go grab a round of shots," Eddie muttered, stepping away from the table.

I took that as my cue to squeeze between the ladies. As soon as I was seated, Poppy leaned into my space with a wide Cheshire cat grin. I'd been hit on enough by forward women to know that while she was definitely brazen in nature, there was nothing sexual or remotely flirty about the energy she was giving off. If anything, it was terrifying.

"So, you're the childhood friend who gets hit on by his students all the time. I bet you have some uncomfortable stories." Something about the way she said it made me think her excitement was more about finding a kindred spirit than finding entertainment in my suffering. Or maybe that was my wishful thinking.

"Yes, that would be me. *Professor Daddy*, apparently," I replied dryly.

"Oh, fuck. Am I going to have a nickname? I don't think I'm comfortable with that," Zack blurted out. *You don't have a choice, buddy.* I held the stray thought in, not wanting to stress the poor guy more than he already was.

Poppy stayed facing me as she rolled her eyes and said, "Nixy, hun. Maybe you should take Zack somewhere where you can focus more on each other, like that racing game you were drooling over."

What was with this lady? I gave Carla a questioning glance and she answered back in a shrug, but she didn't seem bothered by the exchange. *Just go with the flow, Joshua.*

"So pushy," Nixon replied, hopping off his chair. "I'm going to do just that, but because I want to. Be nice to Eddie and Zack's friend."

A devilish smile crossed Poppy's lips as Nixon dragged a flustered Zack away from the table.

"They're cute," I mused as I watched the pair walk off hand in hand.

"Yeah, yeah. Enough of that," Poppy said, waving her hand dismissively. "Quick, before Eddie gets back, how in love is he with Carla?"

Record scratch. That was not where I expected the conversation to go.

Episode 40

The Grand Inquisition

Joshua

I stared at Poppy, then at Carla, who looked absolutely mortified. Okay, so she didn't put her friend up to this, which begged the question why was she asking?

The two watched me closely as I tried to navigate a tactful way of getting out of the conversation. This was dangerous territory for multiple reasons. The last time I talked to Eddie about Carla, he was having a weird internal crisis. *Like you're one to talk.* The point was, I didn't know if he worked through it yet or not. And I couldn't imagine Carla discovering he had panicked over kissing her would help things at all.

"I'm not comfortable talking about this," I said, finally.

"Neither am I," Carla said.

The clear lack of boundaries Miss Pink—excuse me, *Poppy*—displayed for her supposed friends was irritating. Carla was clearly unhappy, frowning as she kept glancing over her shoulder toward Eddie at the bar. *Great.*

He was already in a weird mood, and seeing Carla in distress would tip him over the edge. Eddie was a loyal friend and usually clear-headed, but all reason went out the window when he thought someone important to him was in trouble.

Poppy let out a frustrated huff when she realized I wasn't going to budge.

"He's cockblocking her, which isn't cool. I mean, the other guy is a tool, so I wasn't going to get involved, but it's starting to mess with Carla. If he wants to make a move, then he needs to man up and do it instead of pussyfooting around. And don't try to deny he likes her. He's even got Nixon spying."

I blinked in disbelief at the drama she unloaded on the table. It felt like a mini soap opera in the making.

"Bob's not a tool," Carla argued. How was that the part she latched on to? Poppy scoffed in response, clearly secure in her opinion of Eddie's competition. *Bob in Accounting.*

Ignoring the bickering about Bob the Tool now unfolding, I sat speechless and tried to process the strange info dump. Eddie acting out wasn't that surprising, but the fact that he had someone spying on Carla didn't sit right with me. *At least she seems aware of it?* Still, it didn't excuse the behavior.

Against my better judgment, I let out a breath and gave them something in hopes it would be enough to make Poppy drop it.

"Eddie's never had real feelings for a girl before Carla. He has no point of reference to explain what he's feeling, so he has no idea what's going on in his own head. That's all I'm going to say."

"That makes more sense than I want to admit," Poppy said. Her posture relaxed as she leaned back in her chair, seemingly satisfied with our exchange. *Thank fucking God.*

My phone buzzed in my pocket, giving me the perfect opportunity to nope out of the conversation. Pulling it out and unlocking the screen, I smiled as I read the message from Cassie.

Goddess: I miss you, and I hope you are having fun with whatever you are doing tonight.

Goddess: Here are the links for when you have the time. Be a good boy and read them.

As much as I wasn't keen on checking out those links, it was hard to refuse when she asked like that. *Plus, there will probably be a reward for being such a good boy and obeying.* That thought brought an even bigger smile to my face.

"Text from your girlfriend?" Eddie asked as he arrived at the table with a tray full of shots.

"Jesus, Eddie," I said, startled.

He didn't react, sliding the full tray onto the table. The number of shots was obscene. More than enough to get the table nice and drunk.

"How did you get them to give you a tray? Why didn't the server bring it?" Poppy asked. Both were excellent questions.

"Unimportant," he answered in true Eddie fashion as he handed everyone a shot glass. "Now, tell Cassie I said hi and put your phone away. You'll see her tomorrow."

"Who's Cassie?" Carla asked, not missing a beat.

Eddie didn't answer immediately. Instead, he smiled, handing me a shot before passing each of the ladies. I begrudgingly took mine, desperately hoping for the ground to open up and swallow me whole.

"Stop scowling. Your colleague is gone, and Poppy won't talk. Your secret is safe at this table," Eddie said with a waggle of his brow.

"Why do I not like where this is going?" Carla asked as she furrowed her brow in concern.

Poppy watched me with an amused expression like she knew exactly where the conversation was heading. She'd probably be shoveling popcorn in her mouth while she enjoyed the show, if she had any. Fuck me. There was only one thing to do now. *Bottoms up.* I downed the shot, then grabbed a second one and did the same. The burn of the alcohol wasn't enough to distract me from the knot in the pit of my stomach, but the buzz would soon kick in. That would hopefully numb me enough.

"It's all Eddie's fault," I said, tilting my head toward the ceiling with eyes closed.

"One, I never told you to date her," Eddie said indignantly. "Two, neither of us knew she was a student at the university. And three, you are over the moon for her. Don't play this off like you're mad."

"Oh... no..." Carla whispered.

"That's, um, not surprising from a childhood friend of Eddie's, actually." Something about Poppy's reaction made me snap. I wasn't the kind of man to sleep with my students. *Except you are sleeping with your student.* I've spent my entire career avoiding their advances! *Until now.* No, even now. I was the one who came on to Cassie, not the other way around—goddammit!

"I'm not into the young ones," Eddie protested.

I shot him a glare, my blood boiling below the surface. Was I mad at what he was implying about me or that he was taking a dig at Cassie? Both, probably.

"*I* didn't want to. *You* were the one who pushed me. *She just took a shot, so she is at least twenty-one. We're in Florida. She isn't your student,*" I said, recalling our conversation that night.

All eyes turned to Eddie as he shrugged, unbothered by the attention. "Again, I said fuck her not date her."

He had to be kidding me. Leave it to Eddie to use semantics to try to shift the blame. *Such a salesman thing to do.*

"I take it no one else knows?" Carla asked.

"It's not something I can really go around advertising even if I want to," I replied.

"You want people to know you're dating a student?" Poppy asked with a thin veil of judgment.

"No," I shook my head, "but I want people to know I'm dating her. I...I really like her, and it feels wrong to treat her like a secret."

"You barely know her, and it puts your job at risk," Eddie countered. *No fucking shit*! "But," he continued before I could explode my pent-up frustrations, "she has a surprisingly good head on her shoulders. And she isn't afraid to stand her ground." *If he only knew.*

"Why is this the first I'm hearing about it?" Carla probed.

I shot Eddie a shit-eating grin, knowing damn well why he hadn't said anything about it to her. *Come on, Eddie. Tell Carla how you met Cassie because you burst into my apartment in the middle of the night Saturday. I dare you.*

Eddie grabbed a shot and downed it, shaking off the burn. "I was going to tell you before we had dinner with them tomorrow. I just hadn't figured out a good time since we've been so busy with...*stuff*," he explained.

Stuff? Before I could ask what he was talking about, Carla's skin took on a bright red glow. She quickly grabbed two shots, downing them like a pro. *That is an interesting reaction...*

I looked over at Poppy, who didn't seem surprised in the least. Apparently, I was more out of the loop than I thought.

"Do you actually play games, Professor?" Poppy asked out of the blue.

"Um, pinball?" I answered.

"Perfect. The machines are in the back corner. Come on."

Before I could respond, she grabbed my hand, dragging me out to the arcade.

Episode 41
Cornered

Joshua

"Where are you taking me?" I asked Poppy.

Her grip around my wrist was tight as she dragged me down the rows of machines with their flashing lights and loud music. Really tight. Uncomfortably tight.

"I thought we established that already, to the pinball machines." *Pushy and condescending. Fun.*

"Why?" I planted my feet firmly on the ground, unwilling to take another step without answers.

I loved taking orders from Cassie, but only Cassie. Even if I was into that in a broader sense, I didn't know this woman. Being dragged around by a rude stranger was not on my fun list.

Poppy stopped, letting go as she turned to face me. I swallowed the lump in my throat as her eyes raked over my body, assessing me like I was an adversary. I could handle dodging advances, I had been doing that my entire career, but this was not something I knew how to handle. I had no idea what to do if she became hostile. *Please don't go psycho violent on me.*

Meeting her gaze, I tried to fake confidence. Maybe if she knew I wasn't in a playful mood, she would back down and leave me be. *This is ridiculous. You are a grown-ass man. Turn around and walk back to Eddie and Carla!* Yes, I needed to turn around and walk away like an adult.

"Honest thoughts on your friend," she said, breaking the silent standoff.

Um, okay? As high school as this felt, I couldn't bring myself to walk away. I loathed to admit it, but Eddie had been taking great care of me since the breakup, even if it was care I didn't ask for. Poppy obviously felt some kind of way about Eddie and likely would cause issues between him and Carla. I needed to be a good friend and have his back. *And then walk away to safety.*

"Despite being an idiot about a lot of things, and horrible with personal boundaries, Eddie's a good guy deep down. He's very loyal and means well, despite appearances," I replied. A smile tugged at the corner of her lips as her posture relaxed. *Guess that was the right answer.*

"I figured as much," she said. What did that even mean? As irritating as Eddie could be, he was still my friend, and this conversation wasn't sitting well with me.

"Why do you care? What is your involvement?" I pressed, my *teacher's voice* bleeding through with the hint of an edge.

Poppy raised an eyebrow, then smirked as she shook her head. Any attempt at an authoritative presence was useless as she seemed completely unfazed.

"Until recently, I didn't. Their little 'Will they? Won't they?' was nothing more than a periodic annoyance I could easily ignore. But if

I am going to be dragged into it, I want to make sure I know what I'm dealing with," she explained. If you could call that an explanation. It felt like it only created more questions.

"What do you mean?"

Poppy smiled mischievously as she mimed locking her lips with an invisible key. "Can't tell you. Girl code."

Girl code? I pinched the bridge of my nose and let out a long sigh. Just once I would like to go out and it not become some weird thing. Just once.

"Relax. I don't have it out for your friend. Either of them. As long as the people I care about are okay, then I'm pretty chill. Though I have been known to stir the pot when forced to go out against my will." She gave me a knowing look before continuing her journey through the arcade.

I could relate to being forced out in social settings. That had become Eddie's mission in life since my breakup. But that wasn't why I was here tonight. Zack didn't force me, he asked, and I was genuine when I agreed...though, I was beginning to second-guess my decision.

"And who forced you tonight?" I asked, following along.

"Nixon...and surprisingly Carla, but I'm not mad at her. She had no idea," she replied.

"No idea about what?"

I hadn't meant to say the words out loud and admit she piqued my interest, but there they were. *Blame it on the shots.*

Poppy pivoted, walking backward through the crowd so she could face me. A chill ran down my spine as that smile of hers was back. It was becoming clear I was going to have my hands full tonight.

"We need to get better acquainted before I spill my guts, Josh. Tell me a little about you, and I'll tell you about me," she promised.

This was definitely a trap of some sort. She already admitted that she *stirred the pot* when bored, and I was the unlucky victim who caught her eye. *Better you than the happy couples.* That was true. It would give me something to hold over Eddie the next time he tried to push me into something.

"Fine," I acquiesced as we approached our destination.

Something changed in Poppy the moment I agreed. Her playful demeanor vanished as tension I hadn't noticed in her before melted away. For the first time, she flashed me a genuine smile, which left me more on edge after everything. What was going on?

"Thanks for playing along. I really didn't want to be here tonight, so I appreciate it. I'm going to go grab us some drinks."

Before I could respond, Poppy walked off, leaving me more con-fused than ever.

Poppy cackled, holding her sides as she struggled to breathe. I stood at our small table near the pinball machines, watching without amusement as she struggled for breath. She wasn't a bad person once she relaxed.

It took a couple games of pinball and two drinks, but she eventually got me to open up about how I met Cassie. Poppy was nothing if not persistent. It didn't hurt that she eased some of the tension by sharing about herself first.

You would think learning that she dresses up like superheroes would have been the most surprising thing I learned about her, but no, it was that she's Carla's supervisor. The more she talked, the more

I warmed up to the idea. Based on some of the stories she shared, Poppy enjoyed being in control of a situation. *Remind you of someone else?* Tonight was a bit of a nightmare situation for her, but she never fully explained why.

Once I felt comfortable, I wove my tale of heartache turned bad porn script, heavily censoring the obvious parts. I had only gotten as far as my last night in Florida, and Poppy was already giving me a hard time.

"It isn't funny. I broke that poor girl's heart," I said with a frown.

"Sorry, Josh. It just sounds like something out of a sitcom. The waitress you'd been talking to all summer just happens to be waiting outside the bathroom." Poppy wiped a stray tear from the corner of her eye as her breaths started evening out.

Reminiscing about Daphne filled me with a pang of regret. I wish things hadn't ended between us the way they did. It would have been nice to have her as a friend, but when I saw the look in her eyes when I stepped out of that bathroom, I knew it was impossible.

"It's all Eddie's fault," I said.

Poppy narrowed her eyes in my direction as she took a slow sip of her drink. I held her stare, waiting patiently for whatever snarky remark was churning in her head. If giving me sass made her feel better, then whatever.

"Why? Because he *made* you hook up with Cassie?" she asked, the condescension dripping off every word.

I didn't take the bait, keeping my expression neutral as I took a long drink from my glass. This was a game to Poppy—I figured that out after the first drink. She was testing me, piecing together where the line was and when I would push back.

"No. Because he wouldn't stop meddling. Every time I tried to make it clear I didn't see Daphne as more than a friend, he would find a way to undermine me," I replied. "He made damn sure she thought she still had a chance."

Poppy's face fell. I couldn't tell if it was pity or empathy, but I wasn't in the mood for either. Old emotions were surfacing, frustrations I never really dealt with bubbling to the surface.

"I swear, it's like he really thought that I would magically be back to normal if I got laid. Sorry I was heartbroken after the love of my life dumped me." My face twisted in disgust at how sour those last few words felt in my mouth.

Janet wasn't the love of my life, it became clearer and clearer every day that passed. I did love her, but our relationship wasn't what I thought it was. We weren't the leads in some sappy movie who were destined to be, nor were we soulmates. Sure, we could have had a happily ever after, but we didn't, and that didn't mean I would never find love again.

"Aren't you, though?" she asked.

"Aren't I what?" I asked, confused.

"Back to normal... now that you're fucking your student."

I wish. The truth was, I wasn't sure what normal even was anymore. I would never be the same after what I went through.

"No, I'm not. It's actually caused some issues between Cassie and me. At least our roles help smooth some of it out."

I should have felt guilty that I depended on my Goddess for so much of my healing, but she seemed to do the same.

"What? You being the professor in charge?" Poppy asked with a teasing smile.

"The opposite. You're really bad at this," I said, chuckling.

"What? Is she the one in charge? I'll admit, that's new."

It took five seconds for me to realize what I said, the booze already slowing my mental faculties. Why did I say that? How did this woman I just met get me to admit things I hadn't even told my friends?

My eyes dropped to my hands on the table as I tried to push back the onslaught of emotions washing over me. Embarrassment was the strongest at the moment with shame a close second. I didn't want to divulge that kind of information to someone I barely knew, let alone be judged. *What if she tells Carla?* The nausea kicked in with that thought as the large arcade became way too small.

"Listen, forget—" Poppy waved her hand, shushing before I could finish begging for mercy. She wasn't looking at me, her focus set somewhere over my shoulder as the smile on her face disappeared. I turned to see what had her attention, immediately recognizing the two men who approached.

Episode 42
Confessions and Kinks

Joshua

Nixon was practically skipping toward our table, hair disheveled and all smiles. A few steps behind, Zack was much more subdued with a sated look on his face. Neither seemed to care enough to hide the evidence of what they had been up to. *Like you're one to talk.*

"Pops!" Nixon exclaimed as he reached us, throwing his arms around his friend.

Poppy's lips drew into a tight smile as she leaned into the embrace, softly tapping her head to his. *What is with these two?*

"You're on a date, Nixy. Don't be rude," she chided in a gentle voice. There was a weird intimacy at play that I didn't understand, nor did I want to. If I didn't know better, I would have thought they were a couple. *An open relationship, maybe?*

"Looks like you two are getting along well," Zack remarked as he joined us.

"I was going to say the same thing," I said, nodding toward his open fly.

His whole face went crimson as he muttered a curse, quickly rectifying the situation. Nixon cleared his throat as he released Poppy and took a step back, pulling the attention away from Zack. I couldn't tell from his stern expression if he was upset I called Zack out, or if it was something else. I fidgeted uncomfortably as Nixon studied us, his eyes bouncing from Poppy to me and back. It felt like an interrogation without any questions, only judgment. The seconds ticked on as he assessed the situation silently. Seriously, what was this guy's deal?

I glanced toward Zack, but he only offered me a shrug. Did he not find this as strange as I did? *Probably still riding that high after getting his dick sucked.*

Looking back at Nixon, his expression shifted. He was vibrating with excitement as his lips curved into a big, bright smile, filling me with a sense of dread.

"So, I need to find my own ride home?" Nixon asked, wiggling his eyebrows like Eddie.

What? No!

"Yes," Poppy replied, to my surprise. "In fact, we're going to head out. I don't think you two need chaperones anymore."

What the fuck? This was spiraling out of control faster than I could keep up. Where the fuck was Eddie when I actually needed him?

"Nice," Nixon said, shooting me a wink. *No, not nice. Not nice at all.*

Zack shot me a questioning look, but before I could clarify that nothing was going on, Poppy grabbed my hand and pulled me away.

"Have fun, you crazy kids!" Nixon called out as she dragged me through the arcade.

Nope. Nope. Nope. No fun will be had.

There was no way Poppy could have misread the situation. I couldn't have been clearer that I was off the market. Why on earth would she let them think that?

"Mind telling me what you are doing?" I asked curtly as she continued to drag me toward the exit.

"Rescuing you." *Rescuing...me?* That made no sense at all.

We made it two steps outside before I finally had enough of her shenanigans. I would not spend my entire night getting dragged around every time Poppy wanted a change of scenery.

I planted my feet firmly on the ground, causing her to stumble backward with a huff.

"In case it wasn't clear that I have a girlfriend, I'm not sleeping with you," I said.

"No shit. That's why I got you out of there," she replied dryly.

That made no sense at all. Then again, very little of this woman did.

"Come on." She motioned me to follow. "Let me treat you at the diner around the corner. I can fill you in on the way."

The little voice in my head warned me to head back to my car and leave, but my curiosity got the better of me. *Idiot.* Probably, but this was going to bother me all night if I didn't know why. *That's the booze talking.* Poppy flashed me a smile as I nodded. I couldn't drive yet, anyway. May as well get some answers and free food while I sobered up.

"So, how were you rescuing me?" I asked as she led me down the street.

"I know Nixon. He was scheming." He didn't look like he was scheming to me.

"You've got to give me more than that. Right now, you look like the one who's scheming."

She glanced over her shoulder, flashing me a smile. "In a way."

"Keep being cryptic, and I'll just go back."

"Calm your tits, Professor. We're here."

Against my better judgment, I followed Poppy into the diner. It was fairly empty inside, probably because it was still too early for the post-clubbing, drunk crowd. The elderly waitress standing at the front guided us to a booth in the back corner. *Nice and private.* I slid into the seat across from Poppy and stared at her expectantly.

"Fine. Fine. I'll give you answers," she said, rolling her eyes. "I figured if they thought we were going to hook up it would be a win-win. Your colleague wouldn't know about your girlfriend, and Nixon would back off."

"Back off?" Back off who? Me? Her? Both? The guy was just as all over the place as she was. It made sense they were friends.

"Yeah, he was a royal cunt-tease a few nights ago, and it pissed me off. Initially, he was going to try to orchestrate a threesome between me, him, and his date to make up for it."

"Just like that? Do you have threesomes often?" I asked, expecting her to rib me for not catching on to the joke.

Poppy shrugged. "Define often."

Okay, that wasn't the answer I was expecting. Maybe not a joke, then.

"Not all the time," she continued, "but it's happened over the years when one of us is dating someone open to it, or we pick up a stray at the bar we both like."

I stared at Poppy, slowly processing the conversation I walked into. While I never considered myself vanilla in the bedroom before, this conversation, combined with the homework Cassie assigned me, had me reconsidering.

"Anyway, I don't think your friend Zack signed up for something like that. And while he's cute, I don't want to have to convince someone to partake in group sex. Enthusiastic consent, you know?" She tossed me a look like I could actually relate to anything she just said.

Embarrassed and not wanting to make a thing out of it, I nodded along and tried to steer the conversation somewhere safer.

"Um, sure. But then why tag along at all? Couldn't you just lie and say that you are busy?"

Poppy flashed me a lopsided smile before turning her attention to the menu.

"It's complicated."

"It doesn't seem complicated," I replied.

"Says the man sleeping with one of his students," she countered.

"I didn't know she was my student," I argued back. Yes, I was fucking one of my students, but not on purpose!

"But you do now." She gave me a pointed look that made me shrink in my seat.

"I tried to have her drop my class," I said meekly.

"And how did she react?" There was no judgement or sternness in her voice, just genuine curiosity.

I let out a long sigh, casting my eyes toward the table in shame.

"She said no. My options were to have a relationship with her or not, but she wouldn't drop my class," I explained.

The truth was, I could have probably figured out a way to force the issue if I really wanted to. But I didn't want to. Not then and not now. I wanted Cassie, even if it was wrong.

"Sounds complicated." *Touché.*

"You are looking at it all wrong," Poppy said before taking a giant bite of her French toast. She raised a hand to cover her mouth as she chewed, struggling to tame the larger piece.

I pushed the scrambled eggs around with my fork, unable to make eye contact. Talking about kinks with a stranger was not my thing, but the conversation somehow gravitated there, anyway. There wasn't a particular reason for my discomfort. Poppy was great at taking my silent cues when things crossed a line. *That means she bulldozed you earlier on purpose.*

"How do you mean?"

"It sounds like part of your discomfort is from fear of judgment. Who is judging you?" she asked between bites.

The question made me pause. Who *was* judging me? While Eddie knew about Cassie, it was only because he barged his way in. I had been purposely tight-lipped about her so he had no idea what we did. Poppy knew, but she cared more about the age thing than the Domme/sub part, and even then I don't think she actually cared.

"Myself, I guess," I answered with a shrug.

"But why? There is nothing shameful about letting someone boss you around in the bedroom if you are both consenting to everything.

It's not like a professor forcing himself on a student. You are willingly obeying." I rolled my eyes at the cheap shot as Poppy laughed.

"I didn't force her. She forced me," I corrected.

"Sure, sure. But my point is that labels are just words. Calling them something else doesn't change that you enjoy it. Using the correct terms when navigating boundaries can help make sure everyone is on the same page. Your girlfriend is trying to make sure both your needs are being met. Click on the links. If you don't like what they say, tell her."

"You make it sound so easy," I said with a smile.

Poppy raised a brow. "Because it is. You two aren't experimenting with CBT or something."

CBT? I spent all of two seconds debating whether or not to ask what that was, quickly deciding that I really didn't want to know. In the end, she was right. I was pouting because of my own hang-ups about labels. Cassie took the time to listen to my complaints and research solutions. The least I could do is take a look after she put the effort in.

"You're right."

Poppy perked up, giving me a knowing smile.

"Of course I am, Josh. And if you ever have any questions or need to talk, hit me up. I promise to keep it confidential."

Sure.

Episode 43

Meeting Your Boyfriend's Friends

Cassie

I cautiously stepped into the elevator, grateful no one else was around. For some reason, I had it in my head that large sunglasses would be a great disguise. The glances from the other passengers on the bus ride over said otherwise. It didn't help that I had a full backpack, and I kept looking over my shoulder. I couldn't have looked more suspicious if I tried.

Pressing the button to the professor's floor, I let out a long breath as the doors to the elevator closed. *Almost there.* Every muscle in my body felt tight. I couldn't relax until I was in his apartment, away from prying eyes.

I hated sneaking around, not that I hadn't been keeping my relationships a secret from my grandmother since I moved here, but this was different. It wasn't just my grandmother I was hiding from. Introducing Joshua to anyone would be risky.

It could ruin everything you've worked for so far. All the time invested would be wasted. My shoulders sank at the thought.

"Happy thoughts," I muttered to the empty elevator. "He'll assume the worst if he notices you're sad."

I wanted to come over earlier, but brunch with the old bitch took longer than usual. The grandson of one of her friends was in town, and they joined us. It was awful. Not that the guy wasn't attractive, they were always attractive. Unfortunately, good looks were where it ended every time.

Grandmother's latest pick graduated from a prestigious Ivy League school last spring with a major in finance. Most of our conversation was him explaining his investment portfolio at length, the typical mating call of men like him. *Yes, nothing gets me wetter than a man with a square jaw and mutual funds.*

I won't pretend I'm not shallow. I've dated men for their looks in the past. The difference between those situations and every man my grandmother dragged before me was intent. I never entered a relationship expecting marriage as the end goal. Why would I with my whole life ahead of me?

My grandmother was different. She wanted me married off by my freshman year and struggled with the fact that she couldn't make me. The old bitch was so used to being in control that she didn't know how to act in situations where she had no power. She spent the past few years coping by parading every eligible bachelor she could in front of me. What would she think if she knew the truth?

I tightened my grip on my overnight bag as the elevator doors opened. Butterflies fluttered in my stomach. Tonight was different because this wasn't just a sleepover with my professor boyfriend. I was having dinner with his friends. This felt like a big step. Then again, everything with us felt like a big step. After Friday's chat, I was half expecting the professor to pull back completely once the fog of his orgasm lifted. Imagine my surprise, and relief, when the texts started rolling in earlier today. He actually read the links I sent and responded with his thoughts, which were mostly positive. That should have made me excited to see him, but it wasn't just him tonight.

Whose fault is that? Mine, which was why I kept my whining to myself.

Reaching his door, I took in a long breath to steady myself. *This is it.* I barely knocked twice before the door swung open, and an unfamiliar woman greeted me on the other side.

"Hi," I said a little too quickly. My nerves were getting the best of me.

She didn't bother to hide her surprise as she took her time looking me up and down. The butterflies quickly turned to sour milk as I stood in the hallway. I assumed Eddie would have mentioned me, especially since I was the one who suggested they come over, but the weird shock in her eyes had me second-guessing things.

Or she's judging for other reasons...

"Um...I'm Cassie. Joshua invited me," I said, hoping she would let me in.

"Yeah, sorry. I'm Carla," she said, finally moving aside so I could enter. "The guys are in the kitchen."

I nodded, stepping inside and heading straight to Joshua. All I wanted the entire day was to see him.

I could feel Carla's eyes on me as she followed, making my skin crawl. She was hung up on my age. I could tell. Being the youngest one in the room was never pleasant, but this felt worse. It felt natural for friends of my parents or my aunt to regard me as a child, even though I wasn't, but friends of my boyfriend...

"Hey, kiddo!" Eddie greeted me as we entered the kitchen. I shot him a look, and he quickly cleared his throat to correct himself. "Sorry. Hey, Cassie. Better?"

Joshua reached out, pulling me into a warm embrace. I melted into his body. All the stress from the day slowly drained away as the world around us vanished.

"I missed you," he whispered, then planted a kiss on the top of my head.

"I missed you, too. Today was so long and boring. I wish I could have been here hours ago," I quietly confessed.

"Aren't the lovebirds adorable?" Eddie remarked, reminding me we weren't alone.

I stiffened in Joshua's hold, the moment of tranquility gone. This was why Joshua didn't want me to invite them.

"I'm going to drop my bag in the room. I'll be right back." I tried to sound chipper, but it felt forced. *This was your idea.*

Joshua nodded as he hesitantly released me. Touch was important to him when stressed. I couldn't help wondering if something happened before I arrived.

It didn't take long to set my bag down and head back to the kitchen. I thought about hiding out in the room for a bit, but I didn't want to seem rude or make Joshua worry. My feet dragged like lead with each step. I had no idea how to act. What we did when alone was private. I wasn't ready to share that part of us with anyone else, especially when we were still figuring it out.

"I know you warned me, but she's still younger than I was expecting." Carla's voice carried down the hall, causing me to freeze.

Oh my God! Were they really talking about me?

"I'm not the one sleeping with her, sweet cakes," Eddie replied defensively.

My heart sank. Why didn't Joshua stop them? I witnessed him tell Eddie off before so why not now? Because the other woman was here?

"No, but you set them up. Don't get me wrong, I hope this works for you, Joshua, but Jesus, Eddie. What were you thinking?" She sounded like a mother scolding her child. *Bitch.*

The more I listened, the more agitated I became. The way Carla spoke about me, knowing I could walk back in the room at any moment, was insulting. It was like she didn't even care that I could stumble in to hear her talking shit.

The little voice warned me to keep my growing rage silent, but I couldn't. The past few years were filled with too many instances where I let disrespect slide because I felt I had no other option. If I wanted to be taken seriously and not seen as some child, then I needed to take a stand.

"He wasn't thinking. I feel like that's a common occurrence with Eddie. Is it not?" I said, strolling into the kitchen with my head held high and a smile on my face.

Carla snorted a chuckle, the shock of her response deflating some of my anger. She didn't appear the least bit embarrassed I called her out for gossiping behind my back.

"True. What he must have put you through all summer," she said, looking at Joshua.

"Hey," Eddie snapped, frowning at Carla like a kicked puppy.

"Lucky for me he is such a pushy asshole. Almost as pushy as this one," Joshua chimed in as he pulled me back to his side.

I had no words, still confused by the exchange. Maybe this was how they treated each other? Admittedly, Nicole and I would lovingly throw insults when we were alone. It felt weird watching from the outside.

"This is not going to turn into a gang up on me session. Let's eat," Eddie said, a little annoyed.

"See? Pushy," Joshua pretended to whisper, which made Carla burst into laughter.

Things lightened up during dinner. The way Eddie flirted shamelessly with Carla was a sight to behold. It was obvious what he was doing, while also obvious that he had no idea he was doing it. If her attention left him for more than a few seconds, he would find some way to capture it again, whether it was as blatant as hijacking the conversation or something more subtle, like nudging her shoulder. The most amusing of his antics was when he started eating off her plate when she laughed at a joke Joshua made.

Carla was just as hopeless, staring almost constantly at Eddie with a dreamy look in her eyes. He had no reason to be acting like an insecure fool when she was so over the moon for him. How could he not see it?

Joshua squeezed my hand under the table. Judging by the soft smirk curving his lips, he was thinking the same thing.

Leaning in, he brushed a few stray hairs behind my ear and whispered, "They both think they're being sly."

"Ah," I said with a smile.

—❤—

After dinner, we moved to the living room. The room was full of chatter as the three talked at length about topics that didn't interest me in the least. I didn't mind, though. I was content to listen to the soothing hum of Joshua's voice while I sat curled up in his lap, cuddling into his chest.

I loved this side of the professor—calm, confident, and full of life. His hand lightly traced circles on my back as he made some joke that went over my head, but the others broke out into hysterical laughter. He was in his element.

"What about you, Cassie?" Carla asked, pulling me into the conversation.

Crap. I had no idea what the context was since I wasn't really listening to their conversation. "Sorry, I zoned out," I confessed. "What were we talking about?"

"What it was like in college. These two were quite the party animals," she explained.

The idea that Joshua was ever young made me chuckle, though I could definitely see him as the partying type. He *was* drunk Tuesday night, after all. Uptight people didn't get drunk on weeknights. The more I thought about it, the more I wished I could have seen him then. We might have been friends. Maybe we would have had a shot at a normal relationship.

"And you weren't?" I asked, looking at Carla.

"No. I was focused on my studies. I had a plan," she replied, her smile faltering for a second. *Weird.*

"Hey, I had a plan," Eddie interjected. "Don't act like you're so special. I'm also the only one in the group with a house."

Carla rolled her eyes, turning her attention back to me. I had hoped shifting the focus would get me out of answering, but she seemed intent on including me. Maybe it was guilt for her less than welcoming attitude earlier.

"I think my college experience has been pretty average so far." *For someone whose grandmother donates so much money she pretty much runs the place.* "I go to class, hang with friends, but only occasionally party." *Because the old bitch constantly RSVPs me for soirees where she can parade me in front of potential husbands.*

"I know Joshy-boy chose his major because he loves to write. What about you?" Eddie asked, raising a brow.

Why did it feel like I was suddenly under investigation? Wasn't this evening supposed to be about him and Carla?

I shifted uncomfortably in Joshua's lap, less than thrilled where the conversation was heading.

"I enjoy writing, and my mom really wanted me to go to college," I said with a shrug. It wasn't a complete lie. She *did* want me to go to college. They didn't need to know that it was so I could claim an inheritance that would only be bequeathed if I graduated.

"No plans for after?" Carla asked, her brow furrowed. *Judgy much?*

"Not really. I'm taking it one step at a time with the current step being to graduate college on time."

I hated conversations like these. No matter what I said, people always judged, not that I could blame them. I was going to college for all the wrong reasons and getting a free ride from my grandmother in exchange for a lot of my freedom. My whole situation was such a first world problem, but it didn't change how helpless I felt. Lately, I was just riding out the clock so I could have my life back.

"It's getting late, guys," Joshua cut in.

Eddie glanced at his watch and sighed. "Yeah, we should probably get going."

Everyone said their goodbyes as Joshua escorted his friends to the door. Once they were gone and it was just the two of us, a weight lifted and I felt like I could breathe again.

"That was nice," I beamed, finally able to feel happy.

Joshua stared back at me, frowning. "You don't have to lie. It won't hurt my feelings."

Episode 44

After Dinner

Cassie

Joshua's accusation left me speechless. Not that he was wrong, but he wasn't exactly right either. I didn't hate the evening or anything. I just didn't love it. Or Carla. How was I supposed to communicate that without sounding like a bitch when I was the one who invited them?

I stared back at him, lost, unable to form the words I needed to explain what I was feeling. After already causing a few fights, the last thing I wanted was to say the wrong thing.

A few more seconds passed, and it became clear to Joshua that I wasn't in a rush to talk. He let out a sigh as he took a seat next to me on the couch, pulling my feet into his lap. It was such a simple action, but the connection affected us equally, tethering us together so we couldn't drift apart.

"It's okay, you know. Eddie and Janet didn't get along, either," he said as he began massaging one of my feet.

"What?"

"Janet was indifferent at first," he explained, "but Eddie never liked her. He hated it when we started dating again and wasn't shy about it. I'd be lying if I said our friendship didn't suffer because of it. I mean, why would I want to hang out with someone openly disrespecting my partner? Things got a little better when he started bringing Carla along. She was a good buffer for him and Janet, much better at keeping the peace than I was."

My heart broke a little to hear that, not that I was surprised. Eddie did refer to Janet as a disaster when we cleared the air. Who knows what he said to Joshua about her? I couldn't imagine Nicole openly disrespected someone I was dating. Then again, I doubt I would date someone she hated.

"I think Eddie and I are cool," I replied, hoping to relieve some of his worry.

Joshua continued to rub my feet as he flashed me a look that said he wasn't so sure. Who knows, maybe he knew something I didn't, but Eddie seemed pretty sincere when we had our one-on-one. He had no qualms with me as long as I didn't hurt his friend.

"We had a talk the day he took me home. He was honest and respectful about where he stands," I explained, keeping it purposely vague. Joshua stared off into space, mulling over the new information. I could see the struggle in his expression as he tried to fit the pieces together. "Carla gave me a weird look when she opened the door," I finally admitted.

"Wait, what?" Joshua paused, his brows pinch in confusion. The revelation clearly took him by surprise.

"Yeah. It's hard to explain, but it didn't feel great. Then I heard her talking shit about me to you guys. When Eddie does it...I dunno, it doesn't feel malicious. He thinks he's being funny. But after the look she gave me? It just painted everything she did in a weird light. Even when she tried to include me in the conversation after dinner, I questioned whether she was being sincere or looking to point out my age again."

My pulse raced as I unloaded everything I had been holding back, praying he wouldn't take offense. Letting it all out should have been freeing, lifting the burden of my thoughts from me. Instead, I felt anxious as I watched Joshua, waiting for a reaction. I hated waiting. It made me feel so helpless.

"If we keep this going, people are going to have opinions about our age difference. You need to let me know if that's not something you can handle," he replied calmly. His face dropped when I huffed in frustration.

"People can have their opinions, but I would expect our friends to be respectful about it. It also hurts that you didn't speak up." If it had been a stranger, I would have been more aggressive putting them in their place. But Carla was his friend, which meant he should have been the one to shut it down. If he had, I wouldn't have been in that position.

Joshua chuckled, promptly stopping when I shot him a warning look.

"Sorry. I didn't speak up because I didn't think she was insulting you," he replied.

I pulled my feet towards me with a huff. How could he be so blase about her behavior? She had insulted me! Joshua should have been up in arms about her insinuations.

"Cassie, I don't think her issue is what you think it is," he said with a sly smile.

That got my attention. I adjusted my position on the couch so I could lean in closer, curious about what he was trying to say.

"What do you mean?"

"Carla has had a thing for Eddie from day one as far as I can tell. Don't ask me how he's been so oblivious."

"What does that have to do with you and me?" I pressed for clarification, annoyed that he wasn't making any sense.

Joshua laughed like it was obvious. *Ass.*

"Not you and me. You. *Eddie* picked you out."

He watched me, smiling as he waited for it to click into place.

I took a moment to think it over, repeating his words in my head. Eddie picked me out that night. Not Joshua, Eddie...

"If Eddie picked me out, then Eddie thinks I'm attractive?" I said, starting to put the pieces together.

My face scrunched into a sour expression. It never occurred to me that Eddie found me attractive. I mean, it made sense, but it left me feeling gross.

Joshua shrugged. "He's not wrong."

I gave him a playful push before I leaned back and really thought about the revelation. "So, she came after me because she felt threatened? That's dumb."

"Maybe not you, but what you represent. You're young, beautiful, and caught his attention on some level. At least, that's my take. You can never tell with those two."

Joshua took my other foot and continued the massage while I let everything simmer. The simple solution would be to avoid situations where I would see Eddie and Carla, but I didn't want Joshua to feel like he had to choose. That meant that I needed to figure out how to be okay with Carla going forward.

Whatever. They were gone for now, so I was free to put the dinner out of my head and focus on more important things. Things like my sexy professor lovingly massaging my feet. *Thank God I get regular pedicures.*

Joshua looked at ease as he kneaded my foot, his attention drawn to the bright pink polish on my toes. I couldn't help smiling as I watched him lose himself in the task.

"This is how we should spend every Saturday night," I mused, full of contentment.

"With foot rubs?" he asked with a chuckle.

"Among other things." I flashed him a mischievous smile.

Joshua's eyes darkened with desire as he lifted my leg, placing a gentle kiss on my ankle. My body flushed, my own need growing as his lips trailed kisses all the way up to my knee.

"What did my Goddess have in mind?" he asked, knowing exactly what I wanted but obediently waiting for my command. *Good boy.*

"Bedroom. Now."

That's all the instructions the professor needed. He let out a hungry growl as he leapt from the couch, scooping me into his arms. Wrapping my arms around his neck, I threw my head back and giggled with excitement as he rushed us down the hall.

Episode 45

In the Bedroom

Cassie

Who knew fucking your college professor would be so much fun? And I don't mean the sex part, though that was pretty amazing. I'm talking about how he always seemed so excited to fuck me. Like, it wasn't the sex that got him excited; it was sex with me specifically.

Within seconds of entering the bedroom, I had my professor naked on his knees, begging to worship my body.

"I have far too much clothing on," I mused in response as I flashed the professor a wicked smile.

"I think you are right, my sweet Goddess."

Without hesitation, he removed my clothing, tossing the pieces carelessly on the floor around us. There was a frantic hunger he tried to hide behind a playful smile. His throbbing erection, dripping with precum, revealed the truth. My professor wanted to fuck.

Once I was naked and laid out, the professor moved back to his position next to the bed. I scooched to the edge, letting my legs dangle off the side. I loved this position—me sitting upright with the professor kneeling beside me. I felt like a queen.

"Good boy," I praised, giving his head a scratch.

The way Joshua's face lit up warmed something inside of me.

"May I worship my Goddess now?" His eyes blazed with desire.

I nodded slowly, entranced by the hungry gaze that held mine. He didn't break eye contact as he reached out, lifting my ankle to his lips. There was something naughty about the way he watched me as he placed a chaste kiss on my bare skin.

Watching him trail my body with kisses made me realize how much I had been overthinking our relationship. At the end of the day, this was about sex. I didn't need to get to know his friends or meddle in their relationships because what the professor and I had wasn't that deep. We were still getting to know each other, and I kept certain secrets so guarded that there was only so much growth that could happen between us.

The power balance had clouded my perception of things. Our playtime gave us both an outlet to deal with things outside of the relationship, but the relationship itself wasn't that deep. If I could accept what we were, then I could let go of what happened at dinner. I reached down, running my fingers through the professor's salt and pepper hair as he nuzzled against my thigh. The scruff of his neatly trimmed beard scratched at my skin, tickling just a little.

"Make me see stars, Professor," I commanded in a dreamy voice.

A thrill worked its way through my body as Joshua spread my legs and dove in. A fresh wave of arousal coursed through me, warming me as he swirled his tongue around my clit. I fell back on the bed, raising my ass as I threaded my fingers through Joshua's hair, holding him in place. The feel of his mouth on my pussy was electric, sending bolts of pleasure through me. I didn't want it to stop.

Joshua hummed in appreciation as I ground myself into his face, riding the high as he licked and sucked. It felt amazing, but not enough. I wanted more. My pussy was empty, aching to be filled.

"Add your fingers," I moaned.

My professor didn't hesitate, adding one and then two. His tongue lapped at my clit while his fingers thrust inside of me, guiding me to the sweet promisc of release. I felt complete.

A strained moan escaped me, filling the room as my orgasm took hold. Soft waves of pleasure crashed over me as my walls spasmed around his fingers, ebbing slowly as my brain drowned in euphoria. Joshua continued to work my body through the aftershocks, only pulling away when I finally stilled.

A calm flowed over me as my climax receded, leaving me limp and satisfied.

"You're beautiful like this," Joshua said. He slowly crawled up my body, laying his head on my right tit like it was a pillow. I couldn't help giggling at the absurdity as he sighed in contentment.

"Are you saying I'm not beautiful any other time?" I teased.

The professor didn't take the bait, choosing instead to wrap his arms around me in a tight embrace. Our naked bodies pressed together as he continued to use my breast as a pillow, his erection digging into my thigh. We lay like that in silence as the minutes passed by.

My skin prickled with his every breath. The scratch of his beard on my breast was uncomfortable, but I didn't want to break the spell we were under. It was this magic moment in time, a perfect bubble of serenity that I didn't want to pop.

"I hate I can't show you off more," Joshua said, breaking the silence. His fingers traced small circles above my mound as if he was a million miles away in thought as he added, "I don't like hiding you."

For a microsecond, my body stiffened in response, but I quickly relaxed, hoping he didn't notice. I had no words, so I reached out and lightly stroked his hair in response.

I didn't enjoy sneaking around, but even before tonight, I wasn't exactly jumping at the chance to introduce him to my social circle. Stigma of dating your college professor aside, having Joshua meet anyone other than Nicole seemed like a bad idea. It wasn't even about how little he would have in common with them, which was demonstrated quite well by our dinner earlier. I feared his perception of me might change, that he might suddenly see the chasm between our ages and lose interest.

"I like keeping you to myself," I said after a long pause.

"That's not what I meant. I very much enjoy keeping you to myself, too."

The covers beneath us shifted as Joshua adjusted his position. Hovering over me with a look of enchantment, he brushed some of my hair from my face.

"I don't like that you are some dirty little secret," he explained. "You are so much more and you deserve to be treated as such."

I bit my bottom lip, drawing his attention to my mouth. He hummed in approval, leaning down to press his lips to mine. Every kiss between us was nice, but this was different. It was magical with a spark of something heavy that I never felt before. My heart cried when he broke the connection, calming when he placed his forehead gently on mine.

"I know I mentioned it briefly, but come with me to Florida for the winter break. You are too special to be hidden away. Be my date to my friend's wedding. We can make a vacation of it and spend the entire break there."

Two weeks. I had only known the man for two weeks. Any sane person would be screaming to pump the brakes. Making plans for months out in a relationship that was barely old enough to be called one was crazy, and yet the little voice in my head was silent. There was no blaring alarm warning me of danger, no voice screaming about red flags. Nothing.

If I really thought about it, taking a trip to Florida was not a bad idea. My parents were planning on being in Australia this Christmas, and I definitely did not want to spend it with my grandmother. My only other option would be to spend it alone, which wouldn't happen. My grandmother would force Aunt Margaret to retrieve me if she caught wind that I was home alone all break. It was crazy that I was even considering it, but the longer I thought about it, the more it sounded like a great idea. Fuck it, I was going to do this. *Assuming you are still together by then.* Pushing aside the only sliver of doubt in my mind, I pulled Joshua in for another kiss. When we came up for air, he pulled back a little further, giving me a questioning look.

"Is that a yes?" he asked with a grin.

"Yes."

Episode 46
Breakfast

Joshua

The bacon sizzled and popped as its meaty aroma mixed with brown sugar and cardamom, creating a mouthwatering symphony that filled my kitchen. The kitchen timer dinged, signaling it was time to flip the French toast. It was nice to be in the kitchen again, cooking for more than just myself. Watching Cassie enjoy the pizza I made last weekend ignited something inside me that had been dormant since the breakup. I thought before that I enjoyed cooking because it was something Janet and I did together, but now I realized there was more to it than that. I enjoyed that she enjoyed something I made.

My phone buzzed on the kitchen counter as I plated the bacon. After turning off the burner and moving the pan off the heat, I grabbed my phone to find a text from Poppy. She made sure we exchanged numbers after our chat Friday night in case I had any questions. I admit I was skeptical of how helpful she could be, but she proved herself yesterday when she was willing to talk through some of the reading material that Cassie sent.

Poppy: How is Mr. Robinson this morning?

I rolled my eyes at the attempted movie reference, unamused.

Joshua: Making breakfast before she gets up.

Poppy: Aw. How sweet. Someone is looking for praise.

She wasn't wrong. I had been giddy all morning, anticipating Cassie's response. *Maybe she'll even reward me.* That thought sent a thrill through me, my cock hardening in agreement. I wasn't doing this for sex, but I wouldn't turn my Goddess down if she offered.

I placed my phone back on the counter, returning my attention to the food on the stove. The last few pieces of French toast were finished and all that was left was to wake my sweet Goddess.

She looked beautiful, lying on my bed with her long, blonde hair fanned out over the pillow wearing one of my shirts and a pair of knee-high fuzzy socks. My mouth watered as I adjusted my erection so I wasn't pitching an obvious tent. All I wanted to do was crawl between her legs and taste her.

Breakfast will get cold. That wouldn't be good. There was nothing appetizing about cold bacon and soggy French toast.

Crawling onto the bed, I nuzzled into the crook of her neck. The soft moans that escaped Cassie as she stirred were music to my ears.

"Time to wake up. I made breakfast," I whispered.

"Is it morning already?" she asked with a stretch and a yawn.

We cuddled for a moment longer before I coaxed Cassie from my bed. As wonderful as it felt to hold her and ignore the rest of the world, I really didn't want breakfast to spoil after all the work I put into it.

"What smells so delicious?" Cassie asked as she entered the kitchen.

Her compliment had me grinning ear to ear.

"I made French toast, bacon, and oh!" I rushed to the fridge and pulled out a bottle, presenting it proudly. "I also bought champagne and orange juice. For mimosas."

The bright smile on her face was all I needed. She didn't even have to say the words. I knew she was pleased, and that was enough to launch me straight to cloud nine.

"You really went all out. No one has ever done that before."

"Of course not. You've probably been dating guys your age. They wouldn't know the first thing about properly appreciating a woman," I said, only half joking.

"You're right. I should have started dating my teachers years ago," she teased.

The smile immediately dropped from my face as an image of Cassie flirting with another teacher flashed through my mind. I knew she was joking, but it didn't stop the jealousy from slowly creeping in.

Before the feeling could take hold further, Cassie stood on her toes and kissed me. The feel of her lips on mine was all it took to lull me back into a sense of contentment.

"Let's eat," she said as we parted, granting me one of her soft smiles.

"Let's eat," I repeated in agreement.

Cassie insisted on helping me clean the kitchen after breakfast despite my numerous attempts at explaining it wasn't necessary. My original intention was to let everything soak until after she left in the evening, but she was persistent. She was always persistent. And so we stood side by side, enjoying each other's company as we loaded the dishwasher and hand washed anything that wouldn't fit.

"Thank you for reading the links I sent you," Cassie said as she dried a large bowl with the hand towel.

I reached out and took the bowl as I placed a chaste kiss on her head. Everything about our little domestic scene filled me with warmth. It would be heaven to spend every morning like this.

The little voice had to keep reminding me to not get ahead of myself. The relationship was still very new, and even if this did progress into something long term, there was still life. School, jobs, real world obligations, there were plenty of things that would make something like this impossible to carry out day to day. *But a man can dream.*

"Of course. I will admit I wasn't interested at first, but after reading them, I get why you wanted to share them," I said as I put the bowl away.

"I am so glad to hear that! And obviously, not everything in there is for us. Like, I have no intention of being motherly toward you. But it gives us a jumping off point."

I took a moment to watch her standing there full of hope and excitement. The energy radiating off her was infectious.

"And you did a great job taking initiative to research things. That's why you're in charge," I said with a wink.

"I am in charge, aren't I?" she asked with a mischievous smile.

I knew that look. My naughty little Goddess wanted to play. My dick twitched, equally excited for whatever was about to happen.

Cassie stalked toward me with a hungry look in her eyes while I stood frozen, trapped in her spell. It was only a short distance, but a new bolt of pleasure coursed through me with every step she took.

"Aren't I?" she repeated softly as she grabbed my cock through my pants.

My cock answered before I could, growing to full mast in seconds. Cassie raised a brow expectantly as she waited for verbal confirmation, but all the blood rushed south, making it hard to think past the fact that my dick was in her hands. Nothing was hotter than Cassie taking charge. Absolutely nothing.

"Yes...my Goddess," I finally answered.

"*Good boy*," Cassie praised, and I almost came from the excitement. "Now that the kitchen is clean, it's our turn."

Episode 47

Behave

Joshua

My shower was a cramp fit with the two of us in there, but I wasn't dumb enough to say that out loud. Not when Cassie had me against the wall with my cock in her mouth. Only a fool would jeopardize a moment like that. She had me fooled for a moment, insisting that we actually bathe when we first stepped in. I almost pouted, but thought better of it, and was glad I kept my mouth shut when she dropped to her knees. The way she sucked me while the hot water rained down on us made my eyes roll to the back of my head. My body was hers to play with, and it felt like pure bliss.

"Please let me touch you," I begged as my fingers scraped against the bathroom tile behind me.

Cassie had ordered me to keep my hands against the wall, but it was becoming harder to obey. No, that wasn't quite right. I wasn't at risk of acting without permission. I would stand with my hands against the wall for as long as she demanded, but that didn't mean it wasn't torture. All I wanted to do was reach out and tangle my fingers in her wet hair, but she wouldn't indulge me. Or answer me.

"Please, Cassie. Please. Please. Please." My fingers itched to touch her, the desire almost overwhelming as my begging went unanswered.

Being ignored was a strange mix of frustration and arousal. I hated and loved that she was so absorbed with sucking my cock that no matter how much I begged, my needs and desires didn't matter. My only job was to stand in the shower and let my Goddess use my body however she wished.

The way Cassie sucked me with enthusiasm, taking me deeper and deeper until I could feel the back of her throat, felt amazing. No, better than amazing. She felt like heaven. My Goddess was guiding me towards the sweet nirvana of orgasmic oblivion.

My balls tightened as I approached the edge, ready to dive off, while still chanting my desperate pleas to touch her. My impending climax crept closer and closer despite my best efforts to fight it back so I could enjoy the moment even just a little bit longer. Reaching between my legs, Cassie gently cupped my balls, setting off the final chain reaction. My fingers dug into the tile as I roared out in ecstasy, my orgasm bursting through me. Time slowed as wave after wave of intense pleasure crashed over me, driving me to the brink of euphoric insanity. Through it all, Cassie kept working my cock, sucking down every drop of cum.

By the time it was over, I was barely coherent, only vaguely aware of Cassie's movements as she turned off the water and led me out of the shower.

"That was amazing. Thank you," I said.

My head was still swimming as Cassie handed me a towel to dry off. Never had a blow job rocked my world like that. I felt like I said that a lot about Cassie, but there was something about this time. The feeling of powerlessness she incorporated added a new level to things that I was still processing. Not that she hadn't asserted herself when we had been intimate in the past, but this time felt different and I couldn't quite figure out why.

"You're very welcome," she said with a big, bright smile. Fitting since she was my sun, bringing light into the darkness that was my life before her. My whole world had become brighter since she entered i t.

Cassie took a step closer, running her hand down my bare chest. I suddenly remembered how we were both very naked still, neither covering our bodies with a towel. If I could have gotten hard again, I would have been at full mast from the simple connection she created between us. Had I always been so into physical touch?

"Also, I'm proud of you for keeping your hands on the tile like I asked. I'm sure it was hard," she said, praising me in a soft, warm voice.

"It was," I confessed. "I wanted to touch you so badly."

Even now, I still felt the pull to touch her, hold her, wrap my arms around her, but I didn't. The scene may have been over, but things were still so new between us, and I didn't want to risk more fighting when we only had today. I needed to be patient and follow her lead. Cassie would tell me what to do.

"Good boy," she purred as she lightly scratched her nails down my chest. There it was, the words I had been waiting for.

"I think you deserve a reward for following directions so well, even when it got hard," she continued. *A reward?! My Goddess wishes to reward me!* "What would you like to do, Professor? Since you've been such a good boy for me."

"Honestly, I just want to hold you in my arms for a bit," I replied.

Cassie smiled and nodded. "We can do that. Let me just dry my hair a little first."

The rest of the day passed far too quickly. We cuddled and watched some TV for a bit. After lunch, Cassie played around on her phone while I graded some papers. I tried to apologize a few times, but she kept insisting everything was okay and that she understood I had work to do. Her reassurances did little to ease my worry until she forbade me from apologizing about the matter again. It was both amusing and a bit embarrassing.

Then evening came and Cassie had to leave to catch the bus. My heart ached when it was time to say goodbye. I wanted to keep her with me another night, but I knew that wasn't possible for a variety of reasons, most of which were because of our situation. Hell, I couldn't even walk her to the bus stop because someone might see us together. It was frustrating, but I would rather be frustrated and have Cassie than go back to what it was like without her.

Monday was bittersweet. I knew I would see Cassie in the afternoon, but I wouldn't be able to acknowledge her how I wanted to. It hurt because it was only a day ago we were together, really together, and now I was expected to treat her like every other student. But she wasn't every other student. Maybe it was time for a career change. Being a college professor wasn't exactly lucrative. I could always teach high school English, or maybe become a private tutor...except change scared me. Something pretty major would have to happen to make me take that leap. *And being with Cassie isn't?*

"Knock, knock!" Zack called out as he tapped lightly on the open door to my office. "Got a moment?"

"Sure, sure. I got at least thirty minutes before I need to head to my afternoon class," I said as I beckoned him in with my hand. *Thirty more minutes and then I can see her.*

My new friend smiled and nodded, closing the door behind him as he entered the room.

"Thanks. For Friday night, I mean," he said as he took a seat in front of my desk.

"No worries. It was definitely interesting."

"Yeah. Who knew my hookup worked with your friends? What are the chances?" Zack let out an awkward chuckle, seemingly nervous for whatever reason.

"It could have been worse. At least we didn't run into my ex," I said.

That would have been a complete disaster. Not because I wanted her back, I didn't. And not because I wanted answers. Frankly, I couldn't give a shit why at this point. I had mostly moved on since becoming involved with Cassie, so the only thing left was anger. I was mad at the complete lack of courtesy she showed me. For us to have been involved for so long, to break up with me the way she did was disrespectful. If I were to pass her in the street, I would likely explode. Again, not because I wanted her back or wanted answers. I just wanted her to know what a cruel bitch she was. It was strange to have such anger bubbling just under the surface when I still got frustrated every time Eddie complained about her.

"But you said hookup? I thought it was a date?" I tried to redirect my focus to Zack.

He smiled and blushed, dropping his eyes to his folded hands in his lap.

"The evening ended up being more hookup than date," he confessed. His eyes then lifted to mine. "But we do have plans to see each other again."

"That's great." Maybe. I didn't really get to know the guy, Nixon. Based on the picture Poppy unknowingly painted, I wasn't sure I wanted to.

"Yeah. Actually, it's tonight. He invited me over to his place for dinner. Apparently, he loves to cook." I nodded along, but something felt off.

Didn't Poppy mention something that night about threesomes? It was an absurd notion, and yet I couldn't shake the feeling Zack was about to walk into something he wasn't prepared for. Nor Poppy, for that matter.

"Will his roommate be there?" I asked.

"I don't know. I don't think so from how he was talking."

The conversation continued as we moved on to the topic of Saturday night and the little Ainsworth gala. Neither of us was looking forward to it, but Zack was being dodgy about his reasons. I wanted to press him for answers, but my time was running short, and it honestly wasn't my business in the end. After we said our goodbyes, I whipped out my phone to send a quick text. I couldn't let go of the nagging feeling about Zack's little dinner date.

Joshua: I hear Nixon is having company for dinner tonight.

I hit send, a little shocked at how quickly the reply came.

Poppy: Are you serious?

I let out a sigh. While I was glad I listened to the little voice of warning, I was equally sad that I was right.

Joshua: You didn't know?

Poppy: I am going to fucking kill him.

As much as the current situation sucked, it gave me an opportunity to repay Poppy's unconventional kindness. And, if I was being completely honest, entertaining a friend would help keep my mind off my longing.

Joshua: If you don't mind the drive, come to my place for dinner. I could use the distraction.

Poppy: Everything okay?

Joshua: I'm about to see her, but I have to be professional. It's just tough after spending yesterday with her.

Poppy: I'd say sorry, but you did it to yourself.

Poppy: That was out of line. I'm sorry. I'm just pissed now. Dinner sounds great. 7 p.m. okay?

Joshua: Yep. I'll text you the address after I get out of class.

Episode 48

That's New

Joshua

Leaning back casually in my chair, I watched the doorway as my afternoon Creative Writing class slowly trickled in. A few of them acknowledged me with a hello or a nod, the rest were busy in conversations amongst themselves. Pulling up the rear was Cassie, as beautiful as ever, flanked by Jonathan and Valerie. *That's new*, I thought with a frown. Not the Jonathan part. The little prick seemed determined to be the villain in my story, still forcing his presence on Cassie. Valerie was different. I hadn't seen her so much as acknowledge my Goddess's existence before today.

I hated the idea of either of them being close to my Cassie, but something about Valerie's sudden interest sent a chill through me. Blame it on her recent attempts to cross boundaries, but I didn't trust the little suck-up before and I certainly didn't trust her now.

There was no way Valerie could know about Cassie and me, but that only made me more wary. If she were to find out, there was no telling how she would react. Would she lash out at Cassie in a fit of jealousy? Or maybe it would embolden her advances, knowing

I'd already crossed the line with a student. That thought made me shudder. They didn't appear to be friends based on Cassie's less than enthusiastic expression. She looked detached, like her mind was a million miles away while the two nuisances gabbed away, completely oblivious to her disinterest. Not wanting to be caught staring, I diverted my attention to the rest of the class. The last thing I needed was to make the students suspicious. *Or for Valerie to think I was staring at her.* Another shudder ran through me at that thought. No, that was the last thing I needed.

"Seats everyone. We have a lot to cover today," I instructed. It was the best I could do to rescue my Goddess under the current circumstances. Anything more would have drawn unwanted attention since professors normally didn't insert themselves into the trivial day-to-day lives of students.

Everyone took their seats without argument, though Jonathan's eyes did immediately zero in on the back of Cassie's head. I pushed back the twinge of jealousy, reminding myself that him staring a hole in the back of her head didn't change who she belonged to. She was mine, and there wasn't a damn thing he could do about it.

Things would be easier if Cassie was the one enforcing her boundaries, though. While obviously not thrilled to be in conversation with him when she entered, she lacked the confident aura that usually radiated from her. The Cassie I knew stood tall and spoke her mind. She wasn't the reserved shell of a woman who walked into class today.

It hurt to see her like that, probably because it hit so close to home. My own confidence wavered repeatedly throughout my life. Some of the very things that bolstered my self-esteem in high school, such as the constant attention of women, had slowly worn me down over the years. The breakup had made things worse, but with Cassie I felt like the broken pieces of myself were becoming whole again. I wanted to return the favor and see her shine even when I wasn't by her side.

Somehow, I managed to get through my planned lecture without staring at Cassie the entire time. It was a struggle to have her so close and not be able to look her in the eyes or hold her in my arms. Still, it was better than the alternative of not being in her presence at all. One of the side effects of having Cassie in my class was the boost of confidence it gave me when lecturing. For years, I found myself growing increasingly uncomfortable when presenting to a packed lecture hall. In the back of my mind, I was too busy wondering if any of them were undressing me in their heads or preoccupied with lewd fantasies instead of paying attention. There was always a student or two ballsy enough to slip me a very descriptive note letting me know all their dirty thoughts. I hated them and the way they made me feel.

Cassie was different. I didn't mind the thought of her fantasizing about me during class. In fact, I craved it. I held my head high as I paced in front of my desk while I spoke, hoping my Goddess would be impressed. When I leaned against the desk, my shoulders were relaxed and my posture informal, something I never did for my other classes. The smile that crossed Cassie's lips as her eyes followed my every move was the reward I desperately sought, but she wasn't the only one. The entire class was engaged on a level I hadn't experienced in years, and it felt great.

At the end of class, everyone was quick to file out of the room. I was a bit hurt Cassie seemed the most eager, but judging by the way Valerie scurried to follow, I couldn't blame her. I would run out of the room like a bat out of hell, too, if the little redheaded witch was hot on my heels.

As I turned from my desk with my items in hand, I jolted slightly at the sight of a single student who hadn't cleared out with the rest of them.

"Jonathan?"

Episode 49

Anger

Joshua

My lips drew into a strained smile as I tried to mask my irritation. Judging by the hesitant look on Jonathan's face, I was doing a piss-poor job. *Great.*

"Sorry, Professor Grant. I didn't mean to startle you. I just wanted to talk for a second," he said as he approached.

What was with this group? Three out of nine had no regard for office hours. How did the freshmen have a better grasp on procedure than the upperclassmen? Granted, Cassie's bending of the rules was enjoyable, but the others cornering me after class was a trend I did not like one bit.

"Schedule a meeting during my office hours, Jonathan. That's what they're there for," I replied curtly, hoping that would be the end of it.

Unfortunately, my life wasn't that simple. Jonathan froze a few steps in front of me and let out a sigh.

"It's not exactly class related," he confessed.

My muscles tensed as a knot formed in the pit of my stomach. The conversation took a turn I hadn't expected, and I really didn't care to see where it went next.

"Then it's not something we need to discuss, is it?" I replied coldly.

I turned toward the door and took a step forward. Much to my frustration, Jonathan sidestepped, effectively blocking my path.

"Did—did I do something wrong, Professor?" he asked, clearly frustrated himself.

Yes, I thought bitterly, but bit my tongue, knowing I couldn't air my many grievances without putting both Cassie and myself at risk.

"Why do you ask?" I said, not wanting to give anything away.

"I feel like I've offended you somehow. You're very standoffish and sometimes downright aggressive, like the other weekend at the bowling alley. I only wanted to say hello, but you ripped into me and I'm just trying to figure out why." There was a slight shake to his voice as he spoke.

I blinked a few times as I stared at Jonathan in disbelief while he stared back, fighting to maintain eye contact.

"It's nothing personal." *Liar.* "I don't associate with my students outside of class obligations." *Also, technically a lie thanks to a certain beautiful blonde.*

Before Cassie, I avoided fraternizing with students at all costs, even at the few university fundraisers I was occasionally forced to attend. Did I shut down their attempts with the vitriol Jonathan experienced? No, of course not. He was special like that. It didn't change the fact that I was generally uncomfortable in any setting with a student that could open me up to unwanted advances.

"Not even to say hi?"

"No, not even to say hi," I replied with a heated tone, my frustration about to boil over.

"Why?" He continued to push the issue.

The determined look in Jonathan's eyes made it clear he had no intention of just letting this go. If I hadn't despised him before, I certainly did now. Nothing infuriated me more than someone trying to push themselves on me against my will, and that was exactly what this felt like.

Narrowing my gaze, I took in a deep breath, holding it briefly before exhaling. I was the adult in this conversation. If I didn't keep my composure, I was likely to do something that would get me reprimanded.

"Do you know my reputation around campus?" I asked, deciding to change tactics.

"Your reputation?" Jonathan took a step back as he cocked his head to the side and flashed me a questioning look.

"Yes, my reputation. I know you are new to PGU, but I'm sure you've heard the nicknames. God knows none of them are discreet about it."

Recognition gleamed in his eyes for a fraction of a second before a look of guilt washed over his features as his eyes dropped to the floor.

"Yes, I've heard the nicknames," he admitted.

"Of course you have. Everyone has. With that in mind, can you really not understand why I draw such a firm line?"

Jonathan opened his mouth to speak, closing it almost immediately. He repeated the action a few times as he grasped to find whatever pointless words he needed.

"I'm sorry. I wasn't thinking—"

"No, you clearly weren't. Now if you don't mind, I have somewhere to be." I pushed past him.

I didn't actually have anywhere to be, but I was through entertaining Jonathan and his ridiculous grievances. Thankfully, he didn't follow me as I fled.

The more I mulled over his accusation as I walked across campus, the angrier I became. Despite my dislike for him, I had been completely professional in our limited interactions on campus. The only time I openly showed my disdain was the bowling alley. Why did he care about that one interaction so much? It was almost as if the very thought of someone disliking him was a foreign concept he couldn't fathom, which only pissed me off more. What kind of self-deluded fool honestly thought that everyone loved them?

That might explain his obliviousness around Cassie.

The way my body shook with anger, I was actually happy I wouldn't see Cassie again today. She would have known something was wrong, and I didn't want to burden her with my own issues with Jonathan. It seemed like she had enough on her plate with him. Though I wondered what he and Valerie were saying to her before class.

I paused out in the courtyard, stepping to the side of the stone path so I could tap out a quick message to Poppy.

Joshua: Come prepared to drink.

Her answer was almost immediate.

Poppy: That kind of day, huh? I'll grab the good stuff on my way over.

Episode 50

A New Shoulder to Lean on

Joshua

"Kentucky Oak Orgasm?" I said incredulously, reading the label on the bottle of whiskey that Poppy brought over.

The bottle of amber liquid was a decent size and probably cost a pretty penny. The black label attached had a tree with a rather intense expression of pleasure etched in copper ink along with a tongue-in-cheek description.

Poppy leaned against the kitchen counter and gave me a small shrug. "I thought the name was hilarious. Here's hoping it doesn't taste like shit."

The absurdity of her candor made me smirk. I always wondered what kind of person bought their booze based on names and labels. I guess I had my answer.

"Don't give me that look," Poppy warned.

"What look?" I asked innocently, unsure how I offended her so quickly.

"You're judging me!"

"I'm not judging you," I tried to reassure her, but Poppy was having none of it.

She took a step forward and extended her arm, pressing her finger into the center of my chest as she stared me down.

"Don't lie. I see the look on your face."

"Sorry." I raised my hands in surrender. "I didn't realize you were secretly a twelve-year-old boy."

Poppy rolled her eyes and flashed me a sarcastic smile.

"Ha. Ha."

"Seriously, though, thanks for bringing the booze and burgers. You didn't have to do either."

"It's nothing." She took a few steps back as she dismissively waved her hand. "I'm just happy to have somewhere to be other than home."

The playful expression faded from her face as she turned her attention to the white paper bag on the counter and began pulling out the greasy contents. Personally, I would have preferred a chili dog from Sal's over a burger from the Pine Shack, but I wasn't going to complain when I didn't pay.

"Do you want to tell me what's going on? Is Nixon still trying to make a threesome happen?" If Poppy didn't want to talk, I wasn't going to make her, but something was definitely weighing on her.

She turned back toward me and leaned against the counter as she let out a sigh. I waited patiently as her gaze dropped to the ground for a few seconds before rising back up to meet my eyes.

"I don't think he's still trying *that*, but he definitely wants to push some sort of interaction between Zack and me."

"Okay," I said, nodding along, "and that's bad because..."

"How would you feel if your date kept inviting the chick he lived with along?"

"I could see where constantly having a third wheel around would be a problem," I conceded. "In fact, Carla and I had a similar conversation not long ago."

Poppy stared at me and blinked a few times, trying to process my words before giving up and asking.

"You...and Carla?"

"Yeah. When we first got back from Florida, Eddie kept dragging me along every time he hung out with Carla. I thought I was the only one uncomfortable at first, but it turned out she wasn't thrilled either."

"Your friend is an idiot. If he dies alone, he'll have no one to blame but himself."

I gave Poppy a look, unsure where the sudden animosity came from. I could tell from the few interactions I witnessed the other night that she wasn't his biggest fan, but this felt different.

"Did something happen?"

"Yeah, but I'm not airing Carla's business. You might want to check your friend, though."

That's not concerning.

It was almost funny that the man who was so skilled at talking a woman into his bed struggled with all the other aspects of a relationship. Assuming there was a relationship. I wasn't exactly clear about what was going on with him and Carla. They definitely seemed closer when they came over for dinner, but they weren't as overt with their affections as Cassie and I were. Honestly, I had been so preoccupied with Cassie and everything else that it never occurred to me to reach out and set some one-on-one time.

You were never the one to reach out before, the little voice in the back of my mind pointed out. Never was a bit of a stretch, but it wasn't that far from the truth. Eddie was usually the one to plan things like when he called to talk last week, and Cassie ended up being the one he spoke to...

"What about you? You had a pretty rough day judging by your texts," Poppy asked, pulling me out of my thoughts.

"Yeah. There are a few students in my Creative Writing class that are giving me trouble."

"Trouble how? Didn't the semester just start?"

My eyes dropped to the ground as I let out a sigh and nodded. The reminder that we were still only in the first month of the semester filled me with an uneasy dread I hadn't really thought about. If things were already this out of control, how was I going to make it to December?

I was so distracted by my thoughts that I didn't notice Poppy was next to me until she placed a supportive hand on my shoulder.

"Why don't we plate up and pour the whiskey? You can tell me all about it while we eat," she said, offering a soft smile.

I didn't realize how badly I needed someone to talk to until Poppy offered. Janet had taken up so much of my time while we were together that my other friendships fell on the back burner and slowly drifted apart. Eddie was the only person I was still close with, and even that friendship was strained because of my lack of effort.

"That would be great."

Poppy was different from the night we met. She was less manic pixie and more sincere, actively listening as I spoke and asking thoughtful follow-up questions. There were a few points in the conversation where I could tell she was judging me, but she kept whatever snarky comments were floating around in her head to herself.

Our meal was half finished by the time I was done venting about everything, focusing mostly on Valerie and Jonathan. Poppy sat quietly for a moment, chewing the end of a fry, before leaning closer.

"Can I say something and you not get defensive?"

I chuckled, amused that she was basically asking permission to offend me. At least she was trying to be polite about it, I guess.

"I can't promise anything, but I'll try to keep an open mind."

"Fair. It's just, I think you're letting your jealousy cloud your objectivity with the Jonathan guy. Valerie definitely crossed a line, and I think you should do whatever you need to in order to protect yourself, but I think you overreacted with the other guy."

I sat for a moment and soaked in her words. Had I let my feelings toward Jonathan color my interactions with him?

"I've been completely professional during class," I argued calmly.

"Yes, but what about outside of class? You described the bowling alley incident as dressing him down. Do you get confrontational when your other students say hello outside of class?"

The question made me pause and really think about my actions. Had I ever addressed another student like that out in public? The only instance that was even close was my recent altercation with Valerie, but comparing them while calm, even I realized they were two different situations.

"No," I confessed. "Normally, students don't say hello. They cat-call me. I do my best to ignore it because I don't want to reward them with a reaction."

Poppy nodded in understanding.

"Then why didn't you ignore Jonathan? Or at the very least, give him a brief yet professional explanation that you don't converse with students?" Hearing her lay it out like that made me realize maybe I had been treating him unfairly. I was already irritated that night between Eddie dragging me out and the usual catcalling. Then I saw Jonathan hanging out with Cassie in public, something I couldn't do.

"I was mad," I admitted, the shame of my actions washing over me.

"Because he said hi?" The laughter in her voice irked me. I knew she wasn't trying to mock me, but her flippant attitude still hurt.

"No. Because he was with Cassie. Because even if she doesn't want him around, he still has the ability to be in the same social settings with her. I can't do that without risking my job and her reputation," I said bitterly.

The smile instantly dropped from Poppy's face.

"Secret relationships are rough," she agreed softly, the words holding the weight of someone who had experience.

That wasn't quite the response I expected. I was curious to learn more about her experiences, but she didn't look like she was eager to share what she knew. Instead, I took a big bite of my burger and mulled over her words. The new perspective she offered gave me a lot to think about.

Episode 51
After Dinner Discussions

Joshua

The smoky undertones of the amber liquid lingered on my tongue as I sipped my whiskey. It was an interesting flavor that I had grown to enjoy as the evening progressed.

"Penny for your thoughts?" Poppy asked before taking a swig from her own glass.

We sat on the floor of my living room—she leaned against my recliner and I against my couch. I had no idea why we were using my furniture as backrests instead of sitting on them as intended. Poppy plopped herself on the floor first when we moved the conversation here after dinner, and I followed suit to make my guest feel welcome.

"I was thinking about the whiskey you brought. It's good."

The evening had been fairly relaxing overall, very different from when Eddie and I would hang. Poppy listened in earnest, and aside from the occasional oddball comment, most of her advice was pretty sound. It was a welcome change from Eddie's mantra—you just need to get laid.

"Glad you like it. Though, I don't know how you can drink it straight," Poppy said, scrunching her face.

I chuckled softly before looking her in the eyes and taking another sip. That made her do a snort giggle combo that conjured the image of a giant hog trying to laugh. *Better keep that thought to ourselves.*

"And I don't know how you can drown it in pineapple juice." Honestly, what she did was a waste of a good whiskey.

Poppy threw her head back and cackled loudly. I fought back a wince, hoping my neighbors didn't mind the boisterous noise too much. That was the only issue of the night, her tendency to get loud anytime she was excited or amused. *Still better than barging in uninvited.*

Within a few seconds, Poppy calmed down. Her shoulders relaxed as she let out a content sigh.

"I'm surprised you even have pineapple juice," she remarked, "But seriously, it's better than you'd think."

The mood in the room shifted as the smile faded from Poppy's face. She let out another sigh, less happy than before, as she swirled her glass and stared at the liquid with a pensive expression. Something was wrong, that was more than obvious, but I already knew that. The whole reason she came over tonight was because things weren't going well at home for her. I tried to broach the subject a few times earlier, but she was always quick to dodge and pivot the conversation back to me and my problems.

"So...if things go well between the guys tonight, will I be seeing you more often?" I asked, testing the waters. I didn't want Poppy to feel pressured to talk, but I also wanted to make sure she knew I was here if she needed. It was the least I could do after she listened to me vent and wallow.

"Huh?" Poppy blinked a few times and shook her head. "Oh, probably not. Don't get me wrong, you are now unfortunately stuck with me as a friend, but you don't have to worry about me dropping in for dinner every other night."

I tilted my head and gave her an incredulous look. In the small window of time that I knew Poppy, all I had seen her do was avoid Nixon and Zack.

"I'm not opposed to hanging out with them," she insisted before taking another swig of her drink.

"Then why are you here?" I questioned.

"Because I wanted to give them privacy. Once they have a chance to really bond, I won't mind being the third wheel. I'm just afraid Nixon's unintentionally, or maybe intentionally, trying to sabotage things in some misguided attempt to prove his loyalty," she explained.

"Why would he do that?"

Poppy's shoulders slumped as she pulled her knees to her chest, wrapping an arm around them. The sudden need to comfort herself wasn't lost on me, and I found myself worrying that maybe I should have left things alone.

"I think he feels guilty about my breakup a few months back. I knew Nixon didn't like the guy, but he was polite enough once we started dating. What I didn't know was Harrison, my ex, felt extremely threatened by Nixon. I mean, he hid it pretty well."

"What happened?"

"Harrison sat me down and explained how uncomfortable my friendship and living situation made him. The entire conversation blindsided me, honestly. He said I needed to choose. Obviously, I chose Nixon. I can't think of a single situation where I wouldn't."

"Even if they were the love of your life?"

"The love of my life wouldn't ask me to choose," she replied almost instantly.

If I really wanted to, I could have continued poking holes in her logic, but what would have been the point other than to be argumentative for the sake of being argumentative? I didn't entirely agree with her, but I could see her point. The person you were meant to be with would get along with your friends.

I let out a bitter laugh at that realization. Maybe if I had Poppy's view of things, then I could have avoided the whole Janet situation. *But then you wouldn't have met Cassie*, I reminded myself.

My phone started vibrating in my pocket, distracting me from our conversation. When I pulled it out, I was pleased to see the word Goddess on the screen. *Her ears must have been burning.*

Without even thinking, I accepted the call.

"Hello, *Professor*." The lustful purr of her voice made all the blood rush straight to my cock.

The euphoric feeling only lasted a second before I looked over at a very confused Poppy and realized my rude mistake.

"Hi, Cassie. I—"

Before I could finish, Poppy was shrieking with excitement. "Oh my god! Is that her?" She awkwardly crawled next to me, trying not to spill her drink. "It's her, isn't it? Put her on speaker! I want to say hi."

"Is someone there, Joshua?" *Fuck.*

The concern in Cassie's voice made me tense. It never occurred to me how it might look being alone with another woman until that very moment. I cleared my throat and sucked in a breath, steadying my nerves. There was no need to panic.

"Uh, yeah. Poppy. She works with Carla. I met her on Friday night and—"

"Oh, for fuck's sake," Poppy snapped. "Put me on speaker so I can say hello. You're making it sound weird and suspicious."

Cassie giggled, easing some of the tension that was twisting me in knots.

"It's okay. Do as she says," she urged.

It felt like a mistake, but I did as the women wanted and put the call on speaker. *Please don't devolve into utter chaos.*

"Hello, Cassie!" Poppy squealed. "I've heard a lot about you. All good. Better than good, really."

The genuine excitement in her voice caught me off guard. Why was Poppy so happy to speak to Cassie? She had given no indication that she wanted to meet my girlfriend. *Maybe this is her way of being supportive*, I tried to reassure myself.

The other end stayed silent for a moment, making me fear the worst, until my sweet Goddess finally spoke up.

"Hi. Poppy, right? You're a friend of Joshua's?" It was strange to hear Cassie so hesitant and unsure.

"A new friend. We met on Friday when my roommate turned his first date into a circus. Your boyfriend rescued me, twice now," Poppy explained, giving me a wink.

Strange woman. She thinks she's hyping you up.

The way she spoke so naturally, as if the two were old friends, was the complete opposite of Cassie's cautious tone. It made me wonder if I should step in, but for some reason I hesitated, curious to see where it led.

"That's nice. And you know Carla?" The question made me cringe, remembering Cassie's apparent dislike of Carla.

"Yep, I'm her boss," Poppy answered, blissfully unaware.

"Does that mean you know Eddie, too?" Cassie asked.

The smile dropped from Poppy's face as she gave me a look of displeasure. That was a stronger reaction than I had expected. I had to hold back a laugh as I wondered what Eddie would think if he knew his name elicited such a reaction.

"Yes...why do you ask? Has he made you uncomfortable? Joshua, are you letting that ass make her uncomfortable?"

My eyes widened as I tried to figure out how I was suddenly in trouble. That was not where I thought the conversation was going. Stupid Eddie making trouble for me even when he wasn't here.

"What? No! I, um, at least I don't think so," I said, stumbling over my words.

"No," Cassie said, a hint of a smile in her voice. "Eddie is fine. I like him, actually. We have an understanding, I think."

An understanding? Poppy and I exchanged looks. Neither of us liked the way she worded that. *Note to self: ask for clarification later.*

"Yeah, I'm not unpacking that tonight. In fact, it's late and I've got work in the morning. You two lovebirds have fun chatting," Poppy said as she got to her feet.

I stared in disbelief for a moment, more surprised that she was skipping out on a chance to stir the pot than anything. Not that I wasn't grateful she was leaving so I could talk to Cassie, but we were mid conversation when I rudely picked up the phone. The last thing I wanted was for Poppy to feel unwelcome.

"You don't have to go," I said.

Poppy held up her hand and shook her head.

"Nope. Talk to your girl. I know you were missing her today. I'll let myself out," she insisted. That was not what I expected at all.

Before I could argue further, she was heading to the door, calling out one last goodbye before I heard it close.

"She sounds like a lot," Cassie said, making me laugh.

"That she is," I agreed.

Episode 52

At the Gala

Cassie

I sucked in a breath as Nicole delicately pulled the zipper upward, sealing me into my dress. A dull ache settled in my chest as I stared at my reflection in the mirror. All the glitz and glamor was beautiful, but it wasn't me.

"You look fucking hot," Nicole said as she took a step back to admire me.

Somehow I managed a small smile, though we both knew it was forced.

The truth was, I looked better than hot. The blue dress clung to my body in a way that was absolutely sinful. It was obvious it was made to grab men's attention, which was slightly unsettling considering Grandmother picked it out.

"I don't want to look hot." I sulked, letting the smile drop from my face.

"I get it, school function and all, but at least it's better than what you're usually forced to wear. Maybe you can even reuse this one. Take it for a spin when you go out with that older, secret boyfriend."

Nicole was convinced that since he was older, he must be loaded like in all those billionaire romance books. I didn't have the heart to tell her my secret boyfriend didn't make enough to take me to places where evening gowns were the dress code. A bittersweet silence fell between us as I found her eyes in the mirror. Nicole knew how much I hated going to these events. The way Grandmother paraded me around like an accessory was embarrassing, especially when my professors were present. Thankfully, as a third year, I greatly reduced the chance of seeing any of them since Grandmother didn't find the English department to be very interesting to donors.

It was a double-edged sword knowing Professor Grant wouldn't be there. He had become my anchor. His willingness to give me control when no one else would eased the sense of helplessness that seemed to forever consume me since moving out here. I needed that anchor more than ever tonight. At the same time, I was grateful he wouldn't be there. I didn't want him to see me like this. Knock-out dress aside, I was not the goddess he was used to at these things. I was meek and small, trying to garner as little attention as possible. And then there was the fact that I hadn't told him who I was. While nothing I said so far was a lie, I knew it was wrong not to be open about who my grandmother was. The longer I waited, the worse it was going to be, but I couldn't do it. Everyone always treated me differently when they found out. I didn't want *him* to treat me differently.

You have to tell him at some point. I knew that. Keeping it from him was slowly tearing me apart. I thought for sure it would have come up on Wednesday when I hurriedly mentioned at the end of our call that I wouldn't be able to see him Saturday night. To my surprise, he said it was fine and that he had plans as well. That caught me off guard, but I didn't press since I didn't want him to question me either.

"You don't have to go," Nicole whispered beside me. "I could call your aunt and tell her you're sick."

It was a sweet offer, but Grandmother would never believe it. She'd be banging on the door, demanding proof that I wasn't trying to shirk my responsibilities.

"No," I said, shaking my head, "they won't let me off the hook that easily. I just need to suck it up and get through it."

Classical music accompanied by the dull roar of conversation filled the air. The gala was more packed than usual, which meant it was easier to hide in the crowd. Praise God for small miracles. I kept myself tucked behind Grandmother and Aunt Margaret during most of the conversations, slowly sipping a glass of white wine and only speaking when spoken to.

"Lovely event, Agnes. You put on the best fundraisers," one of our current companions praised. I didn't recognize the old woman, which was a bit surprising since I saw all the same faces at these stupid events. It was even more surprising since everyone else currently gathered in our little cluster appeared quite familiar with the mystery lady.

"I couldn't agree more," Beatrice Collins chimed in. "Honestly, they should rename the whole college after you for all that your family has done to support it."

Everyone gave a soft chuckle of agreement as my dear old bitch of a grandmother preened at the praise. These events weren't about helping the school. They were about Grandmother standing in the spotlight while everyone showered her with praise.

"How could I not? The school has done so much for my family. My late husband was an alumnus, as is dear Margaret. And soon my granddaughter, Cassidy, will graduate from this prestigious university," Grandmother said, motioning to me.

My lips drew into a tight smile as I awkwardly acknowledged the small crowd with a nod. *So much for staying in the background.*

"You truly are lucky to have such a blessing," Beatrice said before glancing at her husband, Jasper Collins. "If only we had a child that could have continued our legacy."

The look they exchanged made my blood boil. I raised my glass to my lips and took a quick sip so my thoughts on the matter didn't slip out.

The way they could act like they didn't have a son was infuriating. I'd never met the man, personally, but he was close enough with my mom that I received a card and gift for every birthday and Christmas until I moved out here. He actually lived nearby, but my mom warned me he wouldn't reach out because of his family situation.

"Things are strained between them, Cassie. Worse than your grandmother and I. Take his number for emergencies, but don't expect to run into him otherwise."

I didn't understand how anyone could have a worse relationship with their parents than my mom until I met Beatrice and Jasper. They really pretend they never had a child, and everyone just went along with it.

"Speaking of the future generation," Grandmother said, redirecting the conversation, "I see our recent scholarship student now. Jonathan!"

I held back a wince as she called out to the classmate I had been trying to avoid. Things had only gotten more uncomfortable once he discovered it was my family's scholarship that paid his tuition. It somehow made him more determined to pursue me.

"Mrs. Ainsworth," Jonathan said as he joined our group.

His eager expression strained as his eyes danced over each person in our circle and their extravagant, tailored attire. In only slacks, a button-down shirt, and basic tie, it was obvious how much he didn't belong. If only he knew how much it sucked even when they thought you were one of them.

"This is Jonathan Bailey. He's majoring in creative writing with a minor in linguistics," Grandmother explained as he gave everyone an awkward wave. "I know we usually focus on students who are studying fields that are more practical, but English and the arts are important, too. Why, my dear Cassie is majoring in English."

I stared off into space as Grandmother continued, trying my best to block out her voice. Even when she was trying to be supportive, she came across as condescending. It was absolutely mortifying. Poor Jonathan looked just as lost, smiling and nodding along like every other sentence wasn't a backhanded compliment. An English degree was nonsense in her eyes, but she couldn't say that to her friends. Admitting her granddaughter was pursuing a worthless degree would be a scandal somehow.

"Speaking of the English department, I see one of their professors now," Aunt Margaret announced, "and he's talking to the new history professor. Come, Cassie. Let's go say hello."

Before I knew what was happening, Aunt Margaret had my wrist in a tight hold as she dragged me away from the group. My stomach dropped as I realized he was here, my professor, and we were heading straight for him. *No. No. No. Why?*

I couldn't breathe. Every step closer felt like another weight pressing down on my chest. I tried to plant my feet, but my brain couldn't remember how. It was all happening so fast yet agonizingly slow.

"Joshua, darling! You actually came," Aunt Margaret greeted with far too much excitement. The familiarity in her voice was like acid.

The smile as he saw her was so forced it was painful. I could see the frustration in his eyes as his posture stiffened. She wasn't welcome in his space.

"Hello, Maggie—" Professor Grant's curt greeting cut short as his eyes drifted to me, the smile fading from his face. "Cassie?"

"That's right. My niece is in your class this year. Lucky you," Aunt Margaret said, batting her eyes in his direction like a lovesick moron. *He isn't into you, bitch,* the jealousy screamed through my terror.

"Niece?" Professor Grant's eyes begged for me to say this was some mistake.

I swallowed back the bile rising inside me and let out a shaky breath. Words were impossible. Nothing could stop the panic that was squeezing my throat.

"Yes, niece," my aunt repeated.

This was it, the end of everything that gave me joy—and there was nothing I could do to stop it from crumbling beneath me.

Keep Reading

Don't want to wait for Obedience Volume Three? You can read Episode 53: Doom and Gloom now by subscribing to my Patreon. Subscribers also gain access to exclusive bonus POV episodes not published anywhere else. Patreon.com/lizziebbrown

Also by

Books

The Holiday Pact Duology

<u>Friendsgiving with Benefits</u>
<u>Coming for Christmas</u>

Obedience

<u>Obedience Volume One</u>
<u>Obedience Volume Two</u>

Serials and Other Works

<u>Patreon.com/lizziebbrown</u>